Growing Pains

Growing Pains

Journey Series Book 2

Wanda B. Campbell

MICAH 6:8
BOOKS

Library of Congress Control Number: 2021919571
ISBN 10: 1-956607-02-1
ISBN 13: 978-1-956607-02-4

Cover Design: Tywebbin Creations
Cover Art: Leilani Jimenez

Printed in the United States

Growing Pains
Wanda B. Campbell

Dedication

*This book is dedicated to those willing to fight
through the process to obtain the promise*

Acknowledgments

My Heavenly Father: Thank You for the ministry of writing, and allowing me to speak to Your children.

My husband, lover and friend, **Craig**: I love you way too much. I'm looking forward to discovering the world together.

During the course of writing this book, I lost my mother and eldest brother. Just a reminder of how precious and fragile life is. **Queenie** and **Sam,** I miss you much.

To readers everywhere: Thank you for taking the time.

Stay Blessed!
Wanda B. Campbell

I would love to hear from you at www.wandabcampbell.com and on Facebook in **Wanda B. Campbell Readers & Supporters.**

Chapter 1

Kayla's breathing, which was more like panting, echoed off the bathroom walls sounding like the wind. To calm her nerves as she waited the recommended time, she added pacing to what had become an eight-month ritual. In the beginning, excitement and anticipation flowed from her as she poured the translucent yellow liquid over the white stick-like object and waited for the pink plus sign to appear. Seven times the positive result she desired had evaded her. Disappointment and sometimes anger greeted her instead of the joy only an expecting mother would understand. Despite being given a clean bill of health from her gynecologist, worry about any internal damage the rape she experienced three years prior could have caused had also began to take root.

Samuel, her husband of two years and nineteen days, was in optimum health and dripped testosterone. They were both Christ-followers, and had prayed and both believed it was God's will and time for them to add another child to their family. Kayla loved Danté, the ten-year-old Sam befriended at the youth center where he volunteered. They would gain custody of Danté once his terminally ill mother passed on to glory, but Kayla was ready for a baby now. Samuel, an associate pastor with ambition to establish a church someday, had gone as far as to say God had shown him their baby in a dream one morning. At the announcement, Kayla jumped from the bed and did a victory dance, and then proceeded to throw out the max pack of condoms she'd just purchased two days prior. For eight months she'd been confessing and believing, but still waiting for the manifestation of the prophetic dream.

Samuel, on the other hand, seemed oblivious to Kayla's distress. After every negative test, he'd simply kiss Kayla and say with a mischievous grin, "That means we get to put in more practice." Kayla would respond in kind and give into the unquenchable desire she had for Sam, without voicing her concern. He had no idea Kayla was tracking her temperature and ovulation cycle on a regular basis.

"This time will be different," she whispered, as she stopped pacing and walked over to the marble vanity and picked up the white plastic stick-like object.

"Hey, babe, breakfast is ready," Sam called from the other side of the bathroom door. "I made your favorite, cinnamon French toast and turkey bacon with scrambled eggs and fruit. For a personal touch, I hand-squeezed the orange juice."

Uncontrollable handshaking and sudden heavy tears prevented Kayla from responding.

Sam turned the knob to gain entrance, but couldn't. "I don't know why you still lock the bathroom door. I mean, it's not like I haven't seen every inch of you a hundred times over."

She heard his laughter and wanted to laugh at the absurdity too, but couldn't. The lump in her throat made it difficult to breath.

"Kayla, are you alright? You didn't fall in, did you?"

Kayla reached over and pulled the toilet handle, and then turned the faucet on, hoping to give the impression that she'd been using the toilet and not crying over the sink. Through Sam's teasing, she'd heard his genuine concern. "I'll be right out," she said, after clearing her throat. "I just need to get cleaned up." That was the truth; she needed to brush her teeth and discard the pregnancy test.

"Okay, but don't get too cleaned up. I have plans for you." His voice faded, is if he were walking away from the door.

Kayla didn't doubt Sam's plans would require a hot bath or shower later on. The last time Sam made her breakfast on a Saturday, it took an hour to wash all the chocolate syrup from her body. Even with anxiety threatening to overtake her, the desire to participate in her husband's love games excited Kayla.

After brushing her teeth and tying the garbage bag, Kayla choked back tears and placed a smile on her face that she hoped would hide her inner turmoil, then opened the door and stepped into her bedroom. Turmoil turned into desire the second she saw Sam on their bed waiting for her with a breakfast tray and nothing else. Sam's six-foot-two-inch chocolate frame was simply beautiful, even with the four-inch scar on his lower abdomen. After two years of marriage, Kayla still felt privileged to be the only woman besides Sam's mother to see his bare body. The fact that Sam had saved his virginity for her bestowed on her an honor that at times left her breathless. Due to the rape, Kayla couldn't offer him the same, but Sam was the only man she'd freely given her body.

"Come here, wife," Sam said, while beckoning her with his hands. "I read somewhere that you should eat before engaging in strenuous activity."

"Then I should be fine," Kayla teased, removing her robe. "The only thing on my agenda this morning is more sleep and maybe a small online shopping spree." She sashayed over to the bed and reached over Sam for a piece of turkey bacon, treating him to his favorite view. "Um, this is so good," she flirted, licking her lips.

She chewed slowly, but swallowed hard when Sam moved the tray to the nightstand, and then flipped her back onto the bed.

"If you have the energy to even look at a computer when I'm done, then you can spend as much money as you like."

Her budget-conscience husband's warm breath and lips tickled her neck, and the ministrations of his hands, confirmed it: she could kiss the online shopping spree good-bye.

Chapter 2

S am adjusted his clergy collar then leaned back in the chair and bowed his head. He cherished the solitude of his office every Sunday morning before worship service, using the time to meditate and to spiritually prepare for service. Since Grace Temple reached megachurch status, Sam took his job as Administrative Pastor more seriously. Now that there were literally thousands of souls to watch over, Sam couldn't afford to become lax in his ministerial duties.

After a moment of prayer, Sam raised his head. Immediately, his eyes landed on the wedding photo resting on his desk. Like always, his lips parted into a full-smile. Hands down, aside from his ordination, the day he married Kayla was happiest day in his life. After nearly two years of marriage, Sam couldn't get enough of his Hispanic/African-American curly-haired drama queen. Kayla often shared the humorous story about how Sam literally saved her from drowning, but from Sam's perspective, it was Kayla who saved him. She was the answer to his prayer; the missing part he didn't know he needed.

Before Kayla, although Sam was content, his life was routine and boring. The worst part was he didn't know it until he crossed paths with Kayla Perez. In her unique way, Kayla challenged him to step outside the box he'd built around his life, and in the process took permanent residence in his heart. So far, their life together had surpassed his greatest imagination. The only thing missing was some little Jerrods running around. Sam believed their family would be expanding any day now. If not from biological children, Danté would be joining Sam and Kayla permanently, soon.

Just that quick, the smile evaporated, and Sam's left hand massaged his chest. He'd been trying to massage the ache in his heart every time he thought of Danté Thomas lately. When Sam met the withdrawn and abused little boy over two years ago at the youth center, there was an immediate connection. Danté drew out Sam's paternal instincts, and he instantly fell in love with the seven-year-old. Danté's desire to spend time with Sam over his abusive father, didn't come as a surprise to Sam, but his mother's decision to grant Sam permanent custody of Danté after her demise had blindsided Sam. Yet, the decision to accept the responsibility came naturally. Kayla, who'd already bonded with Danté, agreed without reservation. Danté served as junior groomsman in their wedding. Sam and Kayla moved from their apartment building and purchased a home with space to accommodate Danté. His room was decorated with items Danté selected on visits during spring and summer break. Everything was in place to welcome Danté, but it grieved Sam that the child would have to lose his mother soon in order to join his household.

Sherri Thomas' mother had called last week to say Sherri's condition was deteriorating. On his weekly phone call to Danté, Sam held up a strong front for Danté's sake. Although Sherri had been diagnosed with a severe form of Lupus that had damaged her kidneys and heart, years prior, she'd only recently opted to tell Danté of her prognosis and the real reason they'd moved back to Indiana. After living in California for ten years, Sherri wanted to spend her final days with her parents, back home in Indiana. Sam assumed Sherri procrastinated on telling Danté because he'd already lost his abusive father to the penal system.

Sam sniffled as he recalled the day four months ago when Danté called him crying and begging him to pray for his mother. "Please, tell God to let my mother live," he'd cried into the phone. Sam prayed and then tried to explain that Sherri would be going to a better place where she would no longer suffer. The theological explanation fell on deaf ears and Danté transformed from a playful ten-year-old into a withdrawn paranoid kid.

According to Danté's grandmother, Danté refused to leave his mother's side. She had to threaten him with a whipping to get him to go to school. When he returns, Danté sits in a chair next to his mother's bed and does his homework. He stopped playing outside with friends the day he found out his mother was leaving him. He even gave up his twin bed, opting to sleep in his sleeping bag next to Sherri's bed. On their last Skype chat, Sam thought Danté looked as tired as Sherri, as she struggled to explain to Danté that he would be going to live with Sam and Kayla soon. All of the legal documents were signed and a trust fund was set up.

"Father, please show me how to father Danté and console his wounds," Sam prayed right before Minister Higgins knocked, and then stepped into his office.

"How's life treating you, this fine Sunday morning, Pastor Jerrod?"

Sam smirked at his best friend and accountability partner. Tyrell had asked him that same question every Sunday, since his marriage to Kayla. It eluded more to Sam being able to enjoy the benefits of marriage, than concern about his well-being. "How about I ask you that same question in a few months, Youth Pastor?" Tyrell was engaged to be married in three months.

Tyrell closed the door and sat down in one of the chairs in front of Sam's desk. "I'm sure I'll have a halle-lujah answer for you." Tyrell chuckled, and then leaned back. "Man what's up? I saw you wipe your eyes when I stepped in. Is everything good with Kayla?"

Sam briefly glanced at the wedding picture. "My baby is fine. It's Danté I'm concerned about. It's getting close; I'm expecting the call any day now."

Tyrell's whistle pierced the silence that followed. "Are you ready to take on the role as parent to a hurting pre-adolescent?"

Sam had lost many hours of sleep over that very question. "I've been parenting Danté from afar for two years now, but this transition will be very different. I'm scared to death, but I believe I'm ready. Of course, I'm praying without ceasing."

"What about Kayla? Is she ready?"

"She loves Danté," Sam answered emphatically. "And she's more than ready to start our family." A smile slipped as thoughts of yesterday's playtime crossed his mind.

Tyrell looked down at his watch and then stood to his feet. "I have to go; I'm doing the invocation today. You know I'll be praying for you and Kayla. Parenthood is not easy under the best circumstances."

Following Tyrell's lead, Sam stood and put on his suit jacket. "Appreciate it, man." He grabbed his Bible and followed Tyrell to the sanctuary.

Chapter 3

"Ten more minutes," Kayla mumbled, after looking at the store clock. Ten more minutes, and she'd be off work, and free to set her plan in motion. Kayla loved her position of store manager for a major retail store, but taking inventory and verifying shipments were the last things she wanted to do. Anticipation and excitement gushed from her. How she'd been able to withhold the news of her pregnancy for two days amazed her. She literally bit her tongue twice to keep from spilling the announcement. Although, she'd prayed and hoped for positive results, when the pink plus sign appeared Kayla went into a state of disbelief. After taking another test Saturday evening and three more Sunday after worship service with the same positive results, Kayla was convinced. Finally, a little Jerrod was on the way.

Instead of blurting the news to Sam, Kayla wanted to plan a special evening to give him the confirmation his dream had come true. She also knew the good news would help release some of his stress and worry over Danté. Sam didn't talk about it much, but Kayla knew every night Sam abandoned their bed and paced the floor praying for Danté. While Sam prayed for Danté, Kayla prayed for Sam. Hopefully, after an evening of pampering and aromatherapy along with the news of her pregnancy, Sam would sleep peacefully through the night.

"What are you smiling about?" her assistant manager and friend, Ashley, asked. "Don't answer. If I had a man like Sam at home, I'd be smiling too. Girl, I'd do backflips."

Kayla laughed along with her, and at the same time wondered when her friend had slowed down. Like most product warranties, Ashley operated under a 30-day trial period when it came to men. Nine out of ten times Ashley returned the merchandise for a new and improved model. That is, until she met Bobby Chen Li, the director of the youth center where Sam worked. Bobby, whose birth name was Leroy Jackson, was the perfect match for the runaway church girl.

"Life is great, but I can't tell you how great it is until tomorrow." Kayla rushed the statement out before Ashley bombarded her with questions, and then added, "What are you and Bobby up to tonight?" to distract her.

"Nothing, but I'm trying to convince Leroy to come to Bible Study on Wednesday."

Kayla chuckled. "If you start calling the man by his name, he might show up."

Ashley stopped going through the merchandising diagram and smirked at Kayla. "The man's mama took one look at him and named him Leroy. His birth certificate and his driver's license clearly state his name is Leroy Jackson. That's his name and that's how I'm going to address him. He's only sticking with Bobby Chen Li because he's too proud to admit his latest religious fad didn't pan out. The man just needs to stop running from the Lord. What?" Ashley said when Kayla laughed in her face.

"If that's not a case of the cat calling the kettle black, I don't know what is. Your father is a pastor, and you have been running from the Lord since you learned how to walk. You only slowed down to catch Bobby, but you're still moving."

Ashley closed the binder. "My failure to completely surrender to the Lord is not an excuse for Leroy's identity crisis. When have you ever seen a man from North Carolina, as dark as Leroy, walk around in a Mandarin jacket, high-water pants, and Kung Fu slippers? The man is just plain ridiculous."

"But you're crazy about him," Kayla said, between giggles. "Or just plain crazy."

Ashley quickly sobered. "I do like him a lot and it's kind of scary. This is the first time I've allowed my heart to get entangled since my high school sweetheart. I just wish I knew where this ride will lead."

Kayla moved close to Ashley and placed her arm around her shoulder. "From what I can tell Bobby, I mean, Leroy, is really into you. Why don't you ask God about it and see what He has to say about the possibility of you becoming Mrs. Chen Li." Kayla had to jump back to keep from being hit by the paper Ashley threw at her. "That's my cue to leave," Kayla said, after placing the inventory log on the shelf.

Ashley bent down and retrieved the sheet of paper. "Have a good evening. I'll be here bright and early tomorrow to hear the good news. Don't think I didn't recognize that diversion tactic."

"Yeah, yeah," Kayla mimicked, as she walked out of the storage area. By the time she reached the parking lot she was skipping to the happy music playing inside of her head.

"Perfect," Kayla exclaimed, ninety minutes later after lighting the last candle. She stood back and admired her work. The dining room was set with china to accompany the Thai food she'd picked up from Sam's favorite restaurant. His favorite cider was chilling, and next to his plate was a gift box containing the positive pregnancy test. Soft music played in the background, and the scent of Sam's favorite scented candle permeated every room leading from the dining room to their bedroom. Rose petals marked a trail from the dining room table to the master bathroom, where a hot bath awaited with a massage to follow. With just minutes to spare, Kayla rushed to her room and took a quick shower. The peach-scented body cream barely touched her skin when she heard the garage door open. In record speed, Kayla slid into the pink lace chemise she'd purchased months ago, but had never worn. Believing their first child would be a girl,

Kayla considered the garment befitting for the occasion. Before Sam entered the kitchen through the connecting door from the garage, Kayla slipped into her heels and ran to meet him. Nearly breathless and wearing a big smile Kayla struck a seductive pose against the dining room table.

"Welcome home, love. How was…" she started, but was unable to finish.

"Sherri's mom called. The doctors have given her seventy-two hours to live. I've already booked the red-eye to Chicago. We can rent a car and drive to Indiana from there. Come on, we need to pack. Our flight leaves out of San Francisco, and you know how bad the bridge traffic can be. We can pick up something to eat on the way." Sam brushed past her and continued on to their bedroom.

Kayla watched Sam's retreating back, only a second before the tears began falling.

∞

Kayla stared at the flight attendants while they gave the safety and emergency instructions. She saw their hand movements and their lips move, but she didn't hear one word. She was too busy thanking God they'd made it to the airport in one piece and in time.

She and Sam had planned carefully for this day. They promised Sherri they would be there during her transition to comfort Danté through the process. Sam, the frugal of the two, had purchased open-ended plane tickets and saved enough money to make a spur of the moment trip. Both had given standby notices to their employers and made coverage arrangements. Kayla learned even the most organized plan could throw one off-balance. The past four hours were a blur of discarding the remnants of what was supposed to be a romantic dinner, notifying her regional director and Ashley, calling family members, packing and praying Sam didn't kill them as he weaved in and out of traffic.

She lifted the armrest and reached over and squeezed Sam's hand. They'd made this trip several times before, but this time was different; when they returned they would be parents of a grieving pre-adolescent. "How are you holding up?" Sam had been understandably quiet. Since coming home and making the announcement they must leave at once, Sam hadn't spoken much. He was so focused on getting to Danté, Kayla doubted he noticed the rose petals he tracked around the house or the candles. He'd barely noticed the two cars he almost hit on the freeway on the way to Tyrell's house to drop off their car.

"I'm good." He squeezed back, but his eyes remained focused ahead. "I just want to get to Danté."

"Me too. I can imagine how he feels right now. Losing a parent is hard." Kayla choked back tears. She wanted to be strong for Sam, but the emptiness she felt from losing her father at a young age overwhelmed her.

After the flight attendant checked to see if their seatbelts were fastened properly, Sam placed his arm around Kayla's shoulder and she leaned against his chest.

"Sorry, for ruining the evening you had planned," he said after kissing her forehead.

Kayla's head shot up. "I didn't think you noticed."

"Of course, I did. Pink lace is very becoming on you." He offered her the mischievous grin she'd come to adore, although it lacked its usual passion. "You'll have to model it for me once we get back and settled in." His brows narrowed, as if he were contemplating something. "We'll probably have to cut down on some of our wild activity since we'll be a family of three and Danté is old enough to know how grown folks play."

Kayla's lips smacked and head rolled simultaneously. "We're not cutting back on anything. We'll just have to learn to be creative and maybe a little discreet."

"Discreet is good," Sam said, while rubbing his forehead. Now even knowing how much Kayla enjoyed their lovemaking wasn't enough to relieve his stress, Kayla observed. She rested against his chest once again and prayed for a way to comfort him. It didn't take long for her to find a solution. Being confined in a Boeing 747 surrounded by strangers wasn't the romantic scene she'd envisioned, but it would have to do.

She raised her head and with her fingertips turned Sam's face toward hers. "Honey, you're mistaken about us being a family of three when we return from Indiana." She pressed her fingertips to his lips to quiet him when he motioned to speak. "Actually, we'll be a family of three-point-five for a few months. I'm pregnant," she whispered, after placing his free hand against her abdomen.

Kayla's heart raced and leapt in her chest as her husband's face and demeanor transformed from worry to pure elation. He gestured to remove his seatbelt, but the plane pushed away from the gate and he had to remain seated. Instead, Sam gathered Kayla to him and squeezed her so hard, Kayla thought she'd have a bruise on her shoulder.

After what seemed like forever, Sam released his hold and tipped her chin. "I love you," he said, right before joining their lips.

The quiver in his normal steady lips, revealed to Kayla the depth of his emotions and all that he couldn't verbalize in the presence of strangers. He broke the kiss just as the plane took off. "I guess that pink lace means we're having a girl?" he asked once the plane leveled off.

"Let's see what you have to say after I wear the blue satin."

Much to the displeasure of fellow passengers, Kayla shared hysterical laughter with her husband. She ignored the stares from the rows in front and across from them, and even the flight attendant's stern look. With what lay waiting for them in Indiana, this could be the last laugh they'd have for a while.

Chapter 4

This was Sam and Kayla's fourth trip to Gary, Indiana in the past two years, but unlike on the previous trips Kayla wouldn't have a chance to visit the Jackson 5 Family Home or feed her shopping addiction in the Lake Street Shopping District. She doubted if she'd soak in one ray of sun on Miller Beach, and she didn't care. Since leaving O'Hare Airport, they'd been praying nonstop for Danté.

The text from Sherri's mother had come through as soon as Sam turned his cell phone back on after the plane landed. Sherri was drifting in and out of consciousness, with Danté refusing to leave her side. Under the circumstances, the hospital staff allowed him to lay with her on the hospital bed. According to Sherri's mother, Sherri would attempt to squeeze him every so often. Sam's mother, Stella, who lived in Chicago, was already at the hospital and had confirmed Danté's demeanor.

"Poor baby, he just keeps kissing his mama's cheek and saying, 'Don't go'," Stella had told Kayla over the phone.

Kayla had never been around a dying person before, so she didn't know what to expect. She'd seen dramatic death scenes on television, where the heart monitor suddenly flatlines and beeps consistently until a doctor comes in and turns off the machine. As Sam turned into the hospital's parking lot, Kayla hoped Sherri's transition would be less dramatic for Danté's sake.

Sam held Kayla's hand as they entered the brick hospital structure together, but Kayla had to increase her walking pace to a trot just to keep up with him. During the elevator ride to the third floor, Kayla ceased praying for Danté and prayed for Sam instead. He didn't talk much, but if the worry lines etched on his forehead and downcast eyes were any indication, in a few minutes Sam would not only need her spiritual strength, but physical strength as well. The heavy lean against her body as they exited the elevator proved her assumption.

Kayla and Sam stopped short of entering room 302, and addressed Sherri's relatives, who were standing in the hallway, comforting one another.

"Are we too late?" Kayla asked, louder than she'd meant to.

"No," Sherri's mother answered, before breaking away from her husband. "She's holding on. Barely, but she's still here. Every time she wakes up, she asks have you made it yet." The weariness and pain her voice carried gave Kayla cause to wonder if Sherri's mother would survive losing a child. Her hands clutched a wad of used tissue and a worn Bible.

"Thank God," Sam said, reaching to embrace Sherri's mother. Kayla interpreted Sam's heavy sigh as relief he'd kept his promise to Sherri about being present for Danté in the end. "Where's Danté?" he asked after somberly greeting Sherri's relatives.

"Where else would he be?" Stella Jerrod asked from behind.

Kayla was too focused on Sherri's mother to notice her mother-in-law walk up. "Hey, Mama Stella," Kayla said, in a tone just above a whisper, and then gave her light hug. For the first time ever, Kayla observed Sam address his mother without looking at her or touching her.

"Hey, Mama," he said, but remained focused on the closed hospital room door. "I need to see Danté."

"Go on, baby," Sherri's mother said, and then stepped aside for Sam to enter the room. "He's been asking for you too."

Kayla interlocked arms with Sam, and followed him into the room. Her intentions were to comfort Danté and encourage Sherri, but when Kayla stepped inside and saw the young boy caressing his mother's head against his undeveloped chest, begging her not to leave him, the dam broke. Kayla had to bite her lip to keep from crying out, but nothing could stop the steady flow of tears.

Sherri's eyes were closed and the only sounds permeating the room were Danté's pleas and the rhythmic beat of the machine providing oxygen to Sherri's tired lungs. Sherri had lost weight and her skin was two shades darker due to her failed kidneys.

In three long strides, Sam was at Danté's side stroking his back. "Hey, son. I'm here and so is Kayla."

Danté stopped pleading long enough to tilt his head and acknowledge Sam. "Hey, Dad," he said, and for a brief second, Kayla thought she saw a smile on Danté's face.

Kayla should have been used to Danté addressing Sam as Dad; he'd been doing that since learning his biological father would remain in jail and had given up his parental rights to Danté. Yet, for some reason hearing the endearing term at this time, shredded Kayla's heart even more. She had to lean against the back of the door for support as the weight of knowing the child's time with his mother had dwindled down to hours, maybe even moments. She hoped and prayed Danté wouldn't spend years nursing the loss of a parent like she had. The death of her father had left her bitter and resentful and Kayla didn't want that for Danté.

"Mama, he's here. Sam's here now," Danté said, looking back down at his mother. He then leaned back so Sherri could see Sam.

Sherri's head turned just slightly before her eyes fluttered open. With every ounce of strength, she could summon, Kayla walked over to the bed and stood next to Sam and rested her hand on Danté's shoulder. The content smile on Sherri's face soothed Kayla's heart. Sherri's facial expression spoke the volumes her mouth could not. Sherri was at peace with God and was ready for her heavenly home.

Time stood still for Kayla while Sherri's eyes alternated between her, Sam and Danté. Finally, Sherri nodded and the smile on her face increased slightly. When Sherri's right arm extended with her palm turned upward, Kayla followed Sam's lead and placed her hand in Sherri's. Kayla and Sam held her hand until Sherri beckoned for Danté's hand with her left hand. It was then Kayla noticed Danté's audible pleas had ceased.

With what appeared to be ease, Sherri used her left hand to place Danté's little hand between Kayla and Sam's hands. Once again, Sherri's smile increased, but then her eyes closed. Except for Kayla's occasional sniffles, the group remained stationary and quiet. A peacefulness Kayla couldn't explain had settled in the room, causing Kayla to close her eyes and welcome the calm.

Sam began reciting scripture the second after Sherri's hand went limp. Kayla didn't need to open her eyes to know Sherri was gone. Danté's cries confirmed life for the three of them would never be the same again.

Chapter 5

"Thank you, Jesus." Sam expressed thanks for a safe trip once the airplane came to a complete stop at the gate. The past six days had been chaotic to say the least, but God had kept them safe, and in the midst of death, peace abounded.

Sherri had pre-arranged her memorial service and pre-paid for cremation. She even went as far as to select a keepsake cross and chain for Danté to store a small portion of her ashes and left instructions on where to scatter the rest. Although Sherri's parents held traditional Pentecostal beliefs and didn't like the cremation idea, they honored Sherri's wishes. The memorial service went according to plan without any drama. The exchange of Danté's custody from his grandparents to Sam and Kayla also went according to plan, despite protests from Sherri's siblings who felt Danté should be left in their care. Sherri's siblings knew she had taken out a large life insurance policy after Danté's birth just in case something happened to her.

After Sam produced legal documents granting him and Kayla full custody and making him executive over the trust account Sherri set up for Danté, they backed down.

Financially providing for Danté was the easy part. Trying to fill the void in the child's heart was what frightened Sam. Since a tearful final good-bye kiss on his mother's cheek six days ago inside the hospital room, Danté had remained by Sam's side constantly. Danté opted to stay in the hotel room with Sam and Kayla instead of sleeping at his grandparents' residence. At the memorial service, Danté chose to have Sam and Kayla sit beside him on the first row, opting to receive comfort from Sam, and not his grandparents. During the hour-long service, Danté held his head high and even laughed as funny stories about his mother's younger days were shared. He only cried toward the end, then with maturity beyond his ten years, Danté stood in the chapel's vestibule and thanked everyone for coming as they filed out.

"Your mother would have been very proud of you today. You acted like a mature young man," Sam had told him as they packed Danté's belongings later that evening.

"That's what my mom wanted," Danté responded, but continued packing. "She told me I had to be strong and represent her well, since I was the only thing she'd done right in her life."

Even now as they prepared to deplane, the weight of those words intensified the burden Sam's heart carried. It was too much pressure for a broken ten-year-old to bear.

Finally, I can move my legs. Sam thought the words, instead of voicing them. He didn't want Danté to know how uncomfortable he'd been through the four-hour flight. Danté desired the window seat and insisted Sam sit next to him. Not wanting to disappoint him, Sam forfeited his aisle seat and crammed his long frame into the middle seat without protest. His consolation was the warmth Kayla's body offered resting against him.

After inadequate stretching, Sam sent a text to Tyrell before stepping over Kayla and joining the other passengers in the narrow aisle to retrieve their carry-on luggage from the overhead bin. Danté followed his lead, while Kayla remained seated.

The aisle traffic began to move just as they managed to balance the luggage and Danté's laptop. "Ready?" Sam asked, noticing the melancholy in Danté's facial expression. He exhibited the same sadness as the plane taxied down the runway at O'Hare. Yet, when Danté looked up at Sam, a smile creased his face.

"Sure, Dad. I'm ready to start our new journey together."

Sam hoped his smile conveyed the honor he felt at Danté's total trust in him. If his arms weren't loaded with luggage, Sam would have hugged him. Instead, he gestured his head toward the exit door. "Come on, let's go," he instructed, and then started down the long narrow aisle.

∞

"Did they just leave me?" Kayla asked the question audibly, although she didn't actually expect an answer from the travelers crammed around her. Kayla sympathized with Danté and had taken a back seat and allowed Sam to focus completely on him for the entire week. Inside their hotel room when Danté cried at bedtime, Kayla didn't protest when Sam opted to sleep on the pullout sofa with Danté instead of in the bed with her. Kayla didn't mind Sam comforting the child; she just didn't think Sam would spend every night with Danté, leaving her in bed alone. During the few sit-down meals the three shared, Kayla was excluded from conversation unless Sam asked her to pass him a condiment. Danté rarely addressed her, or acknowledged her presence. The child's wounds were too fresh and deep for Kayla to take Danté's behavior personal, but Sam's inattentiveness bothered her. Kayla wasn't used to sharing Sam to this magnitude. She understood Sam working long hours on church business and counseling sessions, because once Sam came home, he was all hers. That was no longer the case. Raising children wasn't a job that came with regular office hours, and children didn't disappear at the end of the workday.

"Lord, deliver me. I'm jealous of a grieving child," she mumbled, after collecting her purse from the floor below the seat in front of her and maneuvering into the aisle. "Those unstable pregnancy hormones I've heard about must be kicking in early."

By the time she stopped at the restroom and reached the baggage claim turnstile, Sam and Danté were gone and so were most of the passengers. She walked the length of the terminal, checking the other turnstiles without success.

"If they left me, I'm going to kill him," Kayla grumbled, although the thought of Sam leaving his pregnant wife at the airport broke her heart. While Kayla waited for her cell phone to start up so she could call Sam's phone, she considered calling her overprotective brother, Carlos, but decided against it. Carlos beating Sam up wouldn't solve anything and she wasn't a child anymore.

Her neck strained as she scanned the terminal again just in case she'd missed them the first two times before dialing Sam's number.

"Kayla, over here," she heard a voice call, just as Sam's voicemail answered. She disconnected the call and turned to find Tyrell standing near the door, waving her over.

"At least someone remembered me," she mouthed, before starting in his direction.

"Sam and Danté are loading the car," Tyrell explained, once she approached. "We need to hurry before security gives me a ticket." Tyrell placed his hand on her shoulder, a gesture Kayla recognized as his way of rushing her along.

"Sure," she said, and increased her pace with optimism. Sam hadn't forgotten her; he was trying to prevent his friend from getting a ticket. All ill-feelings were erased once she stepped through the sliding door and spotted Sam standing on the curb, holding the front passenger door open for her. He was wearing the crooked grin she adored.

She was denied the opportunity to give into the urge to kiss him when Tyrell said, "Let's get out of here before security comes back."

Before Kayla could take a step, Sam lifted her up and sat her inside the SUV. "Buckle your seatbelt," he instructed before closing the door. Tyrell had merged into traffic before the safety belt clicked into place.

Inwardly, thankful supplication flowed through Kayla as they crossed the new eastern span of the Bay Bridge. As usual, traffic was heavy, but Kayla was glad to be back in the Bay Area. The new adventure awaiting her left her giddy at times, to the point she'd laughed out loud a few times on the plane. She couldn't wait to share with her mother the good news; even Carlos would be excited. She knew she'd be a mother someday, but didn't imagine she'd have two babies in one year. At ten, Danté wasn't a baby, but in Kayla's eyes he was still the cute seven-year-old she'd met three years ago, and if she had her way, Danté and the child in her womb would remain babies forever.

Having maxed out her limit on holding juicy information, Kayla looked over her shoulder into the back seat at Sam. "Did you tell Tyrell the good news?" she asked, when Sam made eye contact.

"I had to. He wouldn't let me load the car until I did," Sam answered.

"Ay that wasn't nice," she said, swatting Tyrell on the arm. "You know your boy tells you everything first."

"What isn't nice?" Tyrell changed lanes before continuing, "He's holding back on my fee. The only thing I charge for these airport runs is a variety tube of Garrett's Popcorn. And I want my stuff."

Kayla shook her head as to clear it. "What are you talking about? Your stuff is in my carry-on, but I was talking about the—"

"The pound cake my mother sent you," Sam interrupted.

"That's what I'm talking about!" Tyrell said, after slapping the steering wheel. "If I was twenty-years older and not already engaged, I'd marry your mama for her cooking." Tyrell laughed and so did Danté.

"What?" Kayla asked, once her head snapped back toward Sam.

"Sweetheart, I know you remember the cake mom packaged and had me stuff into my carry-on."

"Of course." Kayla wanted to say more, but Sam's stern tone sent her into a state of confusion. Why was her husband stuck on popcorn and pound cake? Did he forget she was pregnant? And why was he glaring at her like she'd done something wrong and belonged in timeout?

Kayla had assumed Sam's decision not to tell his mother about her pregnancy during the visit was due to the nature of their visit. Now, she wasn't so sure. By his actions, Sam had just proven he didn't want to discuss the baby. Why, she didn't know. They'd planned the pregnancy together, and not once had Sam resisted participation. So, why the cold reaction?

Without uttering another word, Kayla faced the passenger window, wondering when they'd fallen out of sync.

Chapter 6

From the doorway of Danté's bedroom Kayla asked, "What would you like for dinner?"

He stopped loading the dresser drawer just long enough to shrug his shoulders and mumble, "It doesn't matter. I'll eat whatever you fix." He then continued unpacking as if Kayla wasn't there.

The blasé answer was not what she expected. Danté always clearly expressed his taste preferences without hesitation. He loved Mexican food, and usually got what he wanted. Since Danté entered her life, Kayla had eaten more burritos and tacos than she had her entire childhood.

"It matters to me," she said, stepping fully into the room. His back was to her, but she rested a gentle hand on his shoulder anyway. "I want to make sure your first official night here is enjoyable. You're part of our family now. I want you to feel welcome." The abrupt jerking away and sharp tone threw Kayla even more off-balance.

"Don't make a fuss over me. It's not like I haven't been here before. I'm not a baby. Like I said, I'll eat whatever you fix. My mother taught me to appreciate everything, because people don't have to do anything for you."

Where did that come from, Kayla wanted to ask, but voiced, "I'm not trying to fuss over you, but I enjoy cooking for you and watching you eat."

"You don't have to worry about that now. I can basically feed myself. I'll give Dad a grocery list and he can buy foods I can fix on my own."

Kayla chuckled, thinking the idea absurd. "And just what can your ten-year-old hands fix? Cup O' Noodles? Top Ramen? Or everyone's favorite: a peanut butter and jelly sandwich?"

"I can also bake fish and chicken, and steammed vegetables," he added, with arrogance she hadn't witnessed before. "My mother taught me. I used to cook her food when my grandmother wasn't home. So you don't have to cook for me. I can take care of myself." He stuck his chin out and folded his arms, as if what he'd said was final.

Kayla wasn't sure if she should compliment Danté on his skills, or rebuke him for the attitude in which he expressed them. She decided to wait and review the parenting books she kept in her bedroom before addressing it.

"I'm sure you can take care of yourself, to some degree. However, around here, it's Sam's and my job to take care of you. It's a responsibility I thoroughly

34

enjoy," she added while rubbing his head. "So, what do you want? Beef tacos or turkey burgers?" Narrowing the list down to his favorite items should make the decision easy, or so Kayla thought.

"Neither."

Did he just roll his eyes at me?

"I'll have fried chicken, macaroni and cheese and green beans with biscuits."

Kayla cocked her head sideways. "I don't recall all of that being on the menu. Besides it's too late in the evening to start cooking all that food."

"I don't want *you* to cook." Kayla was right; Danté had rolled his eyes, and now he also smirked. "You can go to Popeyes. I like their food better than yours anyway."

"Excuse me?" Kayla realized she'd yelled, and lowered her voice. "I mean, you never had a problem eating my food before."

Danté stepped beyond her reach before responding, "That's because I didn't want to hurt your feelings. My mother said it wasn't nice to talk about a person's food but, Miss Kayla, you're not the best cook. Maybe Grandma Stella can show you how to cook. I don't want my dad to starve."

Kayla lost count of how many times her jaw dropped and opened again. Who was this kid and what had he done with her sweet Danté? The Danté she knew had never complained about her culinary skills, and he always asked for seconds. And why was he showing a connection with everyone but her? Sam and his mother were "Dad" and "Grandma". She was simply Miss Kayla.

"I'm not going to Popeyes, so you'll just have to settle for tacos," Kayla decided with finality. "Especially, since we just left the grocery store."

"Popeyes? That sounds good," Sam said from the doorway. "Make mine spicy."

Kayla turned and glared at Sam, but didn't utter a word. His earlier behavior in Tyrell's car still troubled her.

"We've had a long day," Sam continued, stepping inside. "Why don't we let someone else do the cooking? With the time difference you must be tired."

Kayla didn't respond to Sam's soft shoulder squeeze. How long had he been standing there, and did he agree with Danté's assessment of her cooking, Kayla wondered. Sam had never complained about her cooking, and he had eaten plenty of it. So had Danté. Was Sam really concerned about her well-being, or did he agree with Danté? What happened to her penny-pinching husband?

"Well, if that's what you want," Kayla conceded. "I'll go pick something up." She ignored the victorious smile on Danté's face and turned to leave.

"Sweetheart, why don't you stay here? Danté and I will go."

More confused and insecure than she recalled ever being about her ability to provide decent meals for her family, Kayla simply nodded and left the room. She went into the kitchen and placed the raw meat inside the refrigerator so it wouldn't spoil, and then went to her bedroom.

Sam and Danté's laughter and jokes as they walked through the house could be heard, but Kayla failed to see any humor. She plopped down on the bed. For the first time Kayla felt like an outsider in her own home.

Chapter 7

S am remained on his knees in prayer longer than usual. This morning he had much to be thankful for; Danté's first official night as his son had gone well. After consuming enough calories and fat at the fast food restaurant to warrant adding five miles to his morning run, he and Danté crashed in the den and watched action movies.

When Sam finally made it to his bedroom, it was after midnight. The second he saw Kayla curled up on her side of the bed, Sam realized he'd forgotten to tell her about the food he'd brought back for her. Kayla hadn't eaten dinner. Not only that, but he hadn't spoken to her after he returned home. After placing the meal box on the countertop, he'd plopped down on the couch in the den and remained there with Danté.

His original plan was to order takeout, but Danté wanted eat at the restaurant. Sam agreed, thinking it would give Kayla some time to rest, but he hadn't meant for her to go to bed hungry. He resolved to make it up to her by making her favorite cinnamon French toast, eggs and sausage for breakfast.

"That won't happen again." Sam made the declaration after standing and stretching. He looked at his watch. If he hurried, he could get in his morning run and cook breakfast before Kayla got up. A brief check in the refrigerator solidified his plan. He'd run an extra mile, and then prepare breakfast for his family.

Ninety minutes later, Sam looked up from whisking eggs and cinnamon to find Kayla standing in the threshold, dressed in workout attire, and holding a water bottle.

"You're up early, considering you're off work today," he said. "I thought you'd sleep in."

"I need to maintain my exercise routine as much as possible. I read that walking is good during pregnancy," she said, while fastening the fanny pack around her waist.

Sam ceased whisking, and after placing the bowl on the counter, walked over and embraced her. She returned the hug, but her grip was lighter and shorter than usual.

"I'm sorry about last night. Danté and I got carried away. I didn't mean to—"

"Don't worry about it," Kayla interrupted, and stepped away. Kayla walked around him, over to the counter and grabbed a banana from the fruit bowl. "I'm sure you guys had fun. I heard y'all in there yelling at the TV. I spent the evening browsing the Internet for baby stuff. I found some really cute things. You wouldn't believe how much is out there."

Sam looked back at the threshold to make sure Danté wasn't near, then moved behind her and wrapped his arms around her waist and kissed her neck. "Sweetheart, about the baby," he whispered in her ear, "I think we should keep it a secret, for now."

Kayla spun around so fast Sam had to lean backward to keep from getting slapped by her ponytail.

"What? Why?"

"Honey, lower your voice," he whispered, then looked back at the threshold.

"Why?" she asked in a softer tone. "Why should we keep the baby a secret? Everyone knows we've been trying for months."

"I know, but let's wait before we start celebrating. Just until things settle down."

"What things?" she whispered back.

"I don't want to hurt Danté. He just lost his mother and I don't want him to think we're trying to replace him. He's vulnerable right now. What he needs right now is to feel secure with his place in our family."

From her prolonged silence, Sam thought maybe Kayla hadn't heard the whispered explanation, but the sudden redness in her caramel cheeks confirmed she had. Normally, her cheeks turned red just before she lost her temper, but this time he didn't get the wrath he'd expected. The hurt flashed quickly, but the pain remained.

"You're asking me to hide our baby and whisper in my own home because of Danté, whom I've always treated as a son?" she asked in a subdued voice. "I've gone out of my way to help him adjust and offer him comfort, even at my inconvenience. But you want me to act like our baby doesn't exist? Just like I didn't exist last night," she said, taking steps backward.

"Sweetheart, that's not what I mean." He reached for her and flinched. For the first, time his wife pushed him away. "I just want Danté to feel secure and comfortable in his new home," he explained.

"When he's secure and comfortable in his new home, ask Danté to show me how to feel secure and comfortable in my old home."

Sam caught the banana Kayla shoved against his chest just before it fell to the floor. "Where are you going? I made breakfast."

Kayla stopped just short of the threshold and yelled over her shoulder, "I'm going somewhere *I* can feel secure and comfortable."

"Kayla, wait!" Sam called out, but Kayla left the kitchen. This was not how Sam wanted the day to start out. And just what did she mean by that last statement? By the time Sam turned off the stove and removed his apron, Kayla had slammed the front door. At first Sam thought she'd gone for her walk, but then he heard the car engine roar from the driveway.

"It smells good in here, Dad." Danté entered the kitchen before Sam could run out and catch Kayla. "Need some help?"

"No, I'll have to clean this mess up all by myself." Sam yielded to defeat once he heard the tires screech. Kayla was gone.

"Don't worry, I'll help you. After we eat, we'll have the kitchen clean in no time."

Sam smiled for Danté's sake, but his confidence wavered. They may rid the kitchen of mess, but what was wrong with Kayla?

Chapter 8

"I wasn't expecting to see you this morning," Rozelle said, before taking a sip of coffee.

Kayla stuffed a piece of turkey sausage into her mouth to stall for time. Her mother had made that statement at least three times since Kayla plopped down on her couch over an hour ago. At the time Kayla's stepfather, Travis, was home, so her mother didn't press her. Now that Travis had left to play golf and Kayla was seated at the kitchen table, she had to come clean.

"I just decided to stop by for breakfast," Kayla stuttered, after chewing the sausage longer than normal.

Rozelle set the coffee cup on the table and smirked. "So you and my son-in-law finally had a real fight. I'm sure whatever it is, y'all will be glued at the hip again by sundown."

Kayla caught herself before she rolled her eyes at her mother. "Mama, you don't understand. I'm so mad at him right now; I don't care if I see him again."

Rozelle laughed out loud. "This is hilarious. I never thought I'd hear you say that. I thought y'all love was deeper than the ocean. At least that's what you used to walk around singing."

Kayla pouted. "It is. I still love him, but today I don't like him very much."

Rozelle leaned forward and took a sip of coffee. "I feel the same way about Travis at least three times a week. Then he does something sweet and I forget all about what made me mad in the first place. Baby, you sound like a typical married woman."

If only her living environment was as simple as her mother's. Rozelle was married to a man who cherished her to the point he waited ten years for her to heal from old scars and accept his marriage proposal. Kayla had thought Sam adored her in the same way, last night and this morning proved differently.

Telling herself she understood Sam's preoccupation with Danté the night before didn't ease the pain she harbored for him excluding her from their first official dinner as a family. What about Danté? His behavior still had her off-kilter. She had to revisit those childrearing books in a hurry.

"I hear you, Ma, but I'm not going to forget this anytime soon," Kayla finally said, thinking of Sam's request to keep their baby a secret.

"You might not forget, but you will forgive." Rozelle patted Kayla's hand. "Whatever it is, the love you share can overcome it. I'm not surprised y'all fell out," she added after another sip of coffee.

Kayla's newfound insecurity forced her on her feet before she could think rationally. "Why? What have you heard?" The words poured out with anxiety.

"Baby, calm down. You always were a drama queen," Rozelle added, shaking her head.

Slowly, Kayla reclaimed her seat, silently scolding herself for overreacting.

"All I'm saying is, you and Sam have had some major changes lately. The time leading up to Danté's arrival has been stressful—working full-time, flying to and from Chicago and trying to provide emotional support for Sherri and Danté. Plus, you're trying to have a baby in the midst of all that. It's not uncommon for couples to lash out at one another in tense situations."

"Lashing out is one thing, but forgetting I exist is another." Kayla pouted and folded her arms.

"What are you talking about?"

Kayla relayed the highlights of the disastrous evening and waited for her mother to validate her anger. Rozelle's laughter came as a surprise.

"I warned your brother about spoiling you and placing you on a pedestal," Rozelle said once she stopped laughing. "Now you can't handle the real world."

"Huh?"

"You are the baby in the family, and a girl. You have always been the center of everyone's attention. Both your brother and I spoiled you, then we passed the baton to Sam. I can see how you think the world revolves around you, but baby, it really doesn't."

Kayla raised her hands in surrender. "Okay, I admit I'm a tad bit spoiled, but this is not about me. This is about Danté's rude behavior and my selfish husband."

Rozelle smirked. "You need to raise those arms again and repent to the Lord for lying."

"What? That's not true." Rozelle hadn't called Kayla a liar since middle school when she'd accused Kayla of smoking cigarettes. Kayla denied the allegation despite the odor permeating from her clothes. Even after Rozelle searched her backpack and found an opened pack of cigarettes, Kayla held to the lie. Back then, Kayla knew she was lying; she didn't believe that to be the case today.

"Baby, Sam's not perfect, but you know for sure he's not selfish. He's just overzealous in his new parenting role. Danté just buried his mother a few days ago. Although Sherri's death was expected, the child is hurting. I mean, the baby watched his mother die. Let's not forget he still has emotional scars from his father's abuse and abandonment. If he's clinging to Sam, that's a good thing. Sam is filling the void his father left."

Kayla sulked in the chair. Every word her mother had spoken was true, but it didn't soothe her pain. She wanted to nurture Danté and fill some of the void left by Sherri. Kayla knew she could never replace Sherri in Danté's heart, but she hoped for the chance. Maybe her expectations were too high. They'd only been back one night.

"Alright, Ma. Danté is hurting and Sam is just trying to provide stability for him." Sam's request to keep her pregnancy a secret replayed in Kayla's head. She wanted so much to share the good news with her mother, but even angry Kayla couldn't bring herself to go against Sam's wishes. If the announcement had a negative affect on Danté, she'd never forgive herself. As much as she didn't want to, Kayla resolved to wait until Sam felt the time was right.

"Sam would rather physically harm himself than to hurt you," Rozelle continued. "I don't expect you to let Sam get away with that little slight, because that's not how I reared you. I taught you to speak your mind and to express how you feel. But don't be too hard on my son-in-law. Sam's a good man, but just like you're learning how to be a wife, he's learning how to be a husband."

"I know."

Kayla picked up another sausage, but placed it back on the plate before it reached her lips. Kayla wasn't hungry anymore. The conversation with her mother had served its purpose. Rozelle had helped her to see the bigger picture. Kayla was no longer angry, but she wasn't quite ready to return home to Sam and Danté just yet.

"I need to get to the marina before the trail gets too crowded," she announced, standing to her feet. "Between the squirrels and the throngs of people, there won't be room to walk." Kayla waited for her mother to ask why she'd planned on walking instead of jogging, but Rozelle didn't ask. Kayla picked up the dirty dishes and walked over to the sink.

Rozelle stood also, after slurping the last bit of coffee. "You may already be too late to avoid that. After y'all get settled into your new routine, Travis and I will have y'all over for dinner along with Carlos and Jasmine."

"How are my big brother and lady Jasmine doing? I haven't seen them in a while, and every time I call Carlos, he's too busy with Jasmine to hang out with me."

Rozelle smiled her approval. "Get used to it. Your big brother is in love. He's stuck on Jasmine, but he's still trying to fight it. According to Jasmine, he's attending the eight a.m. service regularly, but hasn't joined church yet." Rozelle paused and placed a hand on Kayla's shoulder. "You two are a lot alike."

"Whatever, Ma," Kayla said, too embarrassed to recall her days of running from the Lord. "Carlos will come around just like I did in due time."

"I know his time will come. I'm just anxious to see both of my children happy and in love, like I am. Jasmine already told me, she wouldn't commit to Carlos until he has a genuine Damascus Road experience and water baptism."

Mother and daughter chuckled, but Rozelle recovered first.

"I spent too much of my life alone and afraid to love again. I don't want that for y'all. You wake up and go to bed with love every day and night. I want that for Carlos too, but he's as stubborn as your father was."

Kayla planted a soft kiss on Rozelle's cheek. "Don't worry, everything will work out. God's will always prevails." Kayla walked to the front door pondering her last sentence and found a sense of solace. She and Sam had prayed and received several confirmations. It was God's will for her and Sam to raise Danté. They'd had a rocky first night, but they were moving in God's will. They may have a few kinks, but everything would work out.

∞

"Hi, guys." Kayla practically sang the greeting when she entered the house near dinnertime. She hadn't meant to stay out all day long, but after the three-mile walk around the marina, Kayla didn't feel like going home. The visit with her mother had given her comfort. The fresh air energized her. Watching parents play with their children excited her. Instead of returning home, Kayla went to the mall and made a list of items she'd like for her baby. Despite the fact that she hadn't had her first prenatal appointment, Kayla signed up for the baby shower registry at a major retail store.

Sam and Danté were sitting side by side on the couch. Feeling a pang of guilt for leaving the guys to fend for themselves all day, Kayla headed straight for the kitchen.

She heard footsteps enter the kitchen and assumed they belonged to Sam. "Sorry, I took so long," she apologized while tying an apron around her waist. "It won't take long for me to make dinner." She rummaged through the refrigerator in search of ingredients for shrimp tacos.

"Don't worry about it."

It was Sam. He didn't sound agitated, but she felt the need to explain. "I would have called but I forgot my cell phone. The reception is not good at the marina anyway." She thought it best not to mention the baby gift registry.

That was something they'd planned to do together, but Sam wasn't ready and Kayla's patience was thin.

The firm grip around her waist from behind stilled Kayla. Her search for shrimp ceased.

"I know; I saw your phone on your nightstand." Sam's hands traveled up her body and across her shoulders, gently, but firmly turning her around. With ease his fingertips lifted her chin. Before Kayla could voice another explanation, Sam's lips were on hers.

His gentle, yet thorough lip dance coupled with his roaming hands almost made Kayla forget she'd been angry with him at all.

"I'm sorry about last night and this morning. The way I handled the situation wasn't fair to you. In the future I'll try to be more considerate of your feelings."

The whispered words sent a warm tingling sensation against her nose, causing her to turn away and rub it. The words also held a cryptic message, but Kayla couldn't decipher it. Sam was holding her too close for analytical thinking. "Okay and I'll try to be more understanding."

"Don't worry about dinner. Danté and I cooked."

Reflexively, Kayla took a step backward. Did they dislike her cooking that much? "Why did y'all do that?" The sudden quiver in her voice must have given Sam cause for alarm. After closing the gap between them, he wrapped his arms around her and kissed her forehead.

"Nothing's wrong. Remember, you left here angry with me. I have some kissing up to do. Danté offered to help. You do know he was worried about you?"

It took Kayla a moment to realize Sam's question wasn't a rhetorical one. "Why?" she said for lack of a better response under Sam's fixed gaze.

"Sweetheart, you know he adores you. You're like his mother now that Sherri's gone."

Kayla turned away to hide the smirk from Sam. Obviously, the Danté she encountered last night was not the same child Sam fellowshipped with on a daily basis.

Sam grabbed her hand and pulled closer. "Come on, let's eat. Dinner is set up in the dining room. I've been keeping it warm with that buffet server thingy you ordered last year, but never used."

Kayla let the dig about her online shopping fetish pass and followed him into the dining room. "It smells good in here. What did you cook?" she asked once he released her hand at the table.

"One of your favorites." Sam's jovial expression reminded Kayla how much Sam enjoyed cooking for her. "We'll be right back," Sam announced after scooting her chair in.

Kayla looked around the set table and spotted a gold-etched vase—another casualty of her online shopping. The vase appealed even more to her now that it was filled with fresh-cut multi-colored roses from their front yard. Sam also used the good dishes to set the table. Just as Kayla was about to tip over to the buffet server and sneak a peek, Sam returned with Danté.

"I knew you wouldn't last." Sam teased while filling Kayla's glass with cider.

Kayla eased back down into her chair just in time for Danté to place her favorite salad in front of her. "Thank you," she said, uncertain how the child would respond.

"You're welcome. I made it myself." He sat across from Kayla, but close to Sam.

Danté's proud grin reminded Kayla of the little boy she'd fallen in love with three years ago. "I'm sure it's delicious."

Sam gestured for their hands and said grace. Nearly simultaneously with "Amen" Kayla's fork pierced the baby spinach. She hadn't eaten since Rozelle's house and was starved. She didn't come up for air until the last dried cranberry was gone.

Sam looked toward Danté. "I told you, she would like it."

"My mom would have too."

Fresh sorrow gripped Kayla at Danté's reference to his deceased mother, leaving her guilt-ridden for being angry at the child. She had no idea of his internal struggle. She'd been too young to remember her father, but Danté had ten years of love to reconcile.

Sam patted his shoulder. "I'm sure she would have," Sam acknowledged, then cleared the salad dishes and headed to the buffet server. Danté followed suit. So did Kayla.

"Wow!" Kayla exclaimed from over Danté's shoulder. Sam had made pasta with two types of sauces—Alfredo and marinara, and two types of meat—grilled chicken and shrimp. Her favorites. "Guys, this looks good."

"I'm glad you like it." Sam leaned and tilted his head, like he was expecting a kiss, but his French garlic bread with homemade spread held Kayla's attention.

"I love your garlic bread," Kayla said, just before grabbing a slice and savoring a bite. "Um, this is so good. What?" she asked when Sam and Danté started laughing.

Sam handed her a napkin. "Here, baby. Wipe your face. And slow down, I don't want you to choke before the main course."

Kayla had finished the entire slice in less than three bites and hadn't noticed the crumbs on her chin.

"I wouldn't have to act like a salvage animal if you'd hurry up and feed me," she teasingly joked after taking the napkin. "You know I'm eating for—" She stopped the last word from slipping just in time.

Sam appeared oblivious to her near-slip and scooped her up into his arms and walked back to the table. "I love you even with greasy lips," he muffled the words against her lips before kissing them after placing her back into the chair. "Now stay put."

With renewed adoration, Kayla obeyed her husband's command and watched the males in her life fix her plate. Sam was trying to adjust to the new changes in their lives. Like Rozelle said, Sam was learning how to be a husband. Like her, he didn't always get it right, but his heart was always in the right place. Danté was learning to handle the treacherous blows life had thrown him at a young age, but he cared about Kayla.

She placed her doubts on hold for the night. Sam was trying and Danté was adjusting. She would review those parenting books for sure tonight. Or, maybe in the morning she thought, after mentally disrobing Sam.

Chapter 9

After reviewing his notes for the third time, Sam was satisfied with the plan he'd come up with. In two days, he'd have Danté registered and ready for school. He felt Danté's adjustment would be easier without the dynamics of public school and had secured his enrollment in the private school owned by Grace Temple months prior. He and Danté would ride to and from school and work together. Should an emergency arise, Danté would be within walking distance. Sam's work schedule afforded him the flexibility to ensure Danté would never be left alone, or in the care of strangers.

Kayla's warm body beside him stirred, and when she changed positions, she took most of the blanket with her.

Sam chuckled at his sleeping beauty, and then recovered some of the blanket to cover his now-exposed body. Kayla had always been a cover-hog. With his free left arm, Sam squeezed Kayla briefly and kissed her forehead, then started formulating Danté's daily schedule.

From experience, Sam knew it was impossible to watch a child twenty-four hours a day, but he would try his hardest to be available for Danté. Memories of broken promises from his father to attend special events, or to spend time with him, fueled Sam's desire to be a good father to Danté. Although Sam believed in appropriate spanking, he vowed never to lay a hand on Danté. The child had suffered enough physical pain from his biological father. The childrearing books he and Kayla read had provided clinically proven methods of discipline, but doubted he'd have to use them. Danté was a good kid.

"Since when do you bring work to bed?"

Sam turned his head to find Kayla's eyes half-open. "It's not work," Sam answered, assuming Kayla thought he was preparing for Sunday worship service or Bible Study. "I'm working on our future plans."

Kayla snuggled closer and lifted her head. "Oh really? Let me see."

"Are you sure you're ready to wake up? You gave me quite a workout last night." With hair dangling down one side of her face, Kayla's bright cheeks bloomed red. The fact that Kayla appeared embarrassed at his reference to their lovemaking was hilarious, especially since they'd whispered the entire time, afraid Danté would hear them.

Kayla gathered the sheet around her body and sat up. "I didn't hear any complaints last night."

"And you won't hear any now," he said after brushing her hair back and kissing her lips.

"Let me see this before you distract me again." Kayla reached over his body and took the notebook, causing Sam to kiss the air.

Kayla read the pages in silence, then flipped the pages back, like she was reading them again. "You seem to have everything all figured out." The words came after a prolonged silence and with a hint of sadness. She closed the notebook and placed it on his lap, then faced the opposite wall.

"What's the matter?" Sam turned Kayla's head back toward him. "I thought you'd be proud of our plan. There are some kinks that need to be worked out, but overall it's a good plan." Instead of a verbal answer, tears weld in Kayla's eyes and trickled down her cheeks. "Are you having one of those emotional pregnancy moments?"

Instantly, sadness turned into anger, and Kayla slapped his hand away. "What should I be proud of? The fact that you have methodically written me out of you and Dante's lives, or, that your grand plan doesn't make one mention of our baby?" She pointed at her stomach. "The baby you don't want anyone to know about!"

Sam was at a loss for words, watching Kayla spring from the bed and begin pacing the horizontal length of the bed.

"You have planned Dante's day so precise, you've even factored in mealtimes. You have chores, homework and PlayStation® times down in thirty-minute incre-ments—which I think is stupid. The only thing you don't have scheduled is holding his hand while he uses the bathroom. All that, and not once did you include me, or even ask my opinion. How do you know I don't want to participate in rearing Danté? He does live in my home. How do you know I wasn't willing to adjust my schedule so I could pick him up from school? The way you have it, I can't even make the boy a peanut butter and jelly sandwich. I can't cook anyway, so it doesn't matter."

"What are you talking about?" Sam stood and blocked her path, not caring that his body was exposed. "Of course, you'll participate in rearing Danté. He's our son now."

"No, Sam. Danté is your son. I'm just a person who lives in this house and helps to pay the bills and gets screwed on a regular—in and out of bed."

Sam flinched and took a step backward.

"Just in case you'd like to squeeze us into your micro-managed life," Kayla patted her stomach, "my first prenatal appointment is Wednesday at nine."

Kayla stomped to the bathroom, and Sam followed, but waited for her to finish relieving herself before addressing the insinuation. He also needed to calm his anger. Kayla had no right to accuse him of using her for money and sex. As the product of a strong single mother, Sam valued a woman's worth.

"Why would you say something like that?" he voiced, once Kayla stood at the sink.

Instead of answering him, Kayla brushed her teeth.

Sam's temporal vein pulsated. "Did you hear me?"

"Why did you bother with that pitiful apology last night," she said, once she finished. "Now I fully get it. Being considerate of my feelings doesn't mean I have an opinion in the matter. You'll just inform me for informational purposes. You don't care if I agree or not. If I'd known I was hooking up with a dictator, I wouldn't have married you. Just in case you've forgotten, I lived very well on my own before you, and I can again. I didn't need you then and I don't need you now. You can take your little plan and shove it somewhere." Kayla brushed past him, but then turned around, and in a softer tone asked, "I get why you're so attached to Danté, but why are you so detached from our baby?"

For the first time since his high school days, Sam was afraid to open his mouth. The anger-fueled words he had for Kayla scared him. Never would he have thought the degrading adjectives running through his mind would be directed toward his wife. This was the perfect moment to hold his peace and let the Lord fight his battle. Sam turned away, knowing more than his body was exposed.

"Don't worry Pastor Superdad, I'll give my baby the love you won't." Kayla spat the words just before the door slammed.

Chapter 10

"I can't believe this," Kayla mumbled, from her front row seat during Sunday worship service. As the Administrative Pastor's wife, she'd draw suspicion if she sat in the back instead of next to Pastor Jerrod. She couldn't let the congregation know peace and harmony had evacuated the Jerrod household. "I'm turning into the people I talk about." Kayla detested what she'd termed "fake church folk". People who paraded around church like they resided perpetually on the mountain top, knowing full well their life was raggedy at best. At the moment, Kayla doubted anyone had a more ragged life than her.

Apparently, Sam shared the same "fake it until you make" philosophy. He led the invocation then got caught up in high praise and worship. Even fell to his knees, while Kayla sat back with her head bowed to keep from scowling at him.

She and Sam hadn't spoken to each other in two days, since he came up with that stupid plan to practically raise

Danté alone and probably give the child some kind of anxiety disorder in the process. They'd slept in the same bed, but didn't touch. At meal time, Kayla opted not to join Sam and Danté in the dining room, remaining in the kitchen instead. When he left the house he didn't tell her, neither did she when she left.

She and Danté shared conversation, but only when he reinstated his independence. The day before Kayla had gotten up early and made him breakfast. She'd made his favorite pancakes, but Danté didn't eat them. "I told you, I can feed myself," he'd snapped, before pushing the plate away, then retrieved a box of cereal from the pantry. "Miss Kayla made you breakfast," he announced to Sam when he entered the kitchen a second later.

Kayla stomped from the kitchen without looking at Sam. If he ate the food she didn't know, and didn't care. Yesterday Sam cooked, and as far as Kayla could tell, Danté didn't have any objections to Sam cooking for him.

Sam's nudge brought Kayla back to the present. Pastor Simmons was at the podium presenting his sermon. Usually they shared Sam's Bible during Sunday service, but today when Sam nudged her, Kayla reached underneath the seat and pulled out her own Bible. She turned to the text without ever acknowledging her husband. Sam's heavy sigh in response gave her some sense of satisfaction, but not as much as his expression when she opted out of praying with him for the congregation during the invitation to receive Christ. Anger directed at Sam was a new emotion for Kayla, yet she adapted to it with ease. He'd hurt her and if being disrespectful and contrary made him feel her pain, then so be it. She'd repent to the Lord later for slacking up on the prayer ministry.

After the benediction, instead of greeting congregants alongside Sam at the end of the aisle, Kayla remained seated. She figured Sam wouldn't notice her absence anyway; as always his shadow, Danté was right beside him. The two looked like the perfect father and son, in matching gray suits.

Her earlier victories dissipated, as she watched countless people approach and greet the pair. Danté had been to Grace Temple on many occasions, but now he was officially part of the Administrative Pastor's family, which meant hugs and special attention from the congregation. Kayla had received the same attention when she and Sam became engaged. Back then, she liked the special attention. Today, she didn't.

Pastor Simmons had preached about the Old Testament leader, Gideon, and how God always equips us for battle when we're obedient and place our trust in him. The theory may have held true for Gideon and his three-hundred men, but Kayla couldn't buy into the concept at the moment.

She'd trusted God when she accepted Sam's marriage proposal, knowing he and Danté came as a package. She loved Danté fully and accepted him as her own. On his visits, she'd arranged her schedule to make sure Danté was taken care of. Up until Sherri's death, she thought Danté cared about her. Not once had Kayla considered Sam would exclude her. From the beginning they'd always done everything as a threesome. Now Danté pushed her away, and spoke nice-nasty words when Sam was out of earshot.

"What's up, mija?"

Kayla didn't have to turn around to know who'd addressed her. Only her brother, Carlos called her by the Spanish term. She swallowed the lump in her throat and forced a smile before turning around to address her overprotective brother.

"Hey, dude." She hugged him briefly. "I didn't expect to see you here today."

Carlos smirked. "For real? You know Jasmine has me on a strict worship service and Bible Study regimen. If I don't come to church, I can't see her."

Kayla laughed at Carlos' poor attempt at pouting. "I've never seen you submissive. I'm lovin' the way Jasmine has you under control." Carlos' temporal vein began twitching, reminding Kayla how much he hated being controlled by anyone.

"Mija!"

Kayla tried to shush him before he caught the attention of those lingering in the sanctuary, but failed. Sam along with several other members paused from their conversations and looked in their direction. Kayla and Sam made brief eye contact, and then Sam continued his conversation.

Kayla bit her lower lip to camouflage the hurt the simple gesture caused. Sam always came to her rescue whenever Carlos displayed anger or aggression toward her.

"You know I'm just teasing," she said, interlocking her arm with his. "It's just that I've never seen you so attached to any female. Even mama can't make you do something you don't want to do."

The lines across his forehead relaxed. "Jasmine is special, but she doesn't control me. I mean I like her more than I probably should, but she's pretty special." His tight lips curved into a smile. "I mean, she's not a friend-with-benefits kind of girl. I guess if I ever were to settle down…" he let the statement hang.

Kayla squealed just before slapping her hand over her mouth. "Oh, my goodness, you love her! I can't believe it, my brother is in love."

He shushed her. "Don't say that out loud. Someone might hear you," Carlos said, looking around.

"Someone, like Jasmine?" Teasing Carlos about his budding relationship gave Kayla a reprieve from her stale one. "I promise not to tell anyone, but you should probably let Jasmine know how you really feel."

Carlos ran his hand through his thick hair, something he did when frustrated. "She knows I care about her. I would tell her how much, but I'd have to commit to God first."

Kayla laughed aloud. Watching her tougher-than-nails brother turn into mush was hilarious. "Is that such as hard thing?"

Carlos looked over his shoulder and side to side, like he was checking to see if Jasmine was nearby. "Honestly, I get that I'm not in control of my life and I acknowledge I need a savior, but it's hard for me to accept the 'God as Father' concept when I didn't have a natural father. I was only five when Dad died and Mama didn't date until I was in high school. I was the man of the house. I don't know what it's like to submit to another man, even if it's a divine being. And that whole concept about the man being the spiritual covering for his household, I don't know enough about the Bible to fill those shoes. Even if I accepted Jesus as my Lord and Savior right now, it would take me years to catch up with Jasmine's spirituality." Carlos sniffled and turned away.

Carlos' admission nearly floored Kayla. Observing her big brother's true emotions was a new experience. Carlos often labeled guys who openly displayed emotions as wimps. Now here he was about to break down in the sanctuary. Kayla wanted to hug him and tell him everything would work out; that with God's help he was more than capable of fulfilling the role of husband, but Jasmine entered the now-almost-empty sanctuary and was headed their way.

"Just pray about it," she whispered, while rubbing his back. "Tell God exactly how you feel, and He'll direct you. And tell Jasmine. I'll be praying for you too. Now get it together before your boo gets here."

Carlos sniffled a few times, then cleared his throat. He turned around just in time to greet Jasmine.

The adoring gaze that passed between Carlos and Jasmine caused an internal ache in Kayla. She and Sam used to share that same look.

"I'd better go and join my family," Kayla said, after greeting Jasmine.

"Would you like to join us at the soul food buffet?" Jasmine invited. "That might be the most economical way to feed a growing boy."

Kayla laughed to conceal the hurt Danté's rejection had caused. "You're probably right, but I already cooked. You guys have fun and keep it holy," she teased, then darted away.

With each step toward Sam and Danté, Kayla prayed for the strength to endure another evening of feeling like an outsider in her own home.

∞

Sam stood in the patio doorway watching Kayla read the parenting guide with earplugs in her ears. Thoughts of happier times, when they eagerly read the book together, surfaced. They used to cuddle and discuss the author's views on childrearing versus those of their parents. Sam and Kayla both decided although they'd been reared by phenomenal single mothers, they would do things differently with Danté. The task would be easier with two parents and less stressful, they reasoned. So far, for Sam, the plan was working, but Kayla appeared to have aborted the mission.

The wounds of her verbal attack were still fresh. How could she ever accuse him of using her and not caring about their baby? Why couldn't she recognize he was only fulfilling his role as head of household? It was his responsibility to provide direction and order for the family. What did she mean, she didn't need him? She couldn't possibly think he'd allow her to take his baby and raise it alone.

Replaying the conversation reinforced his position— Sam didn't want to talk to Kayla, but after the empty experience in church today, he had to. Sam had never *faked* his way through service as he'd done today. He'd waved, clapped, sang and even prayed for people, all while being consumed with hurt and anger. He forced countless smiles and pretended to be interested in the lives of the people around him, when in reality he wasn't paying attention.

However, he had paid attention to Pastor Simmons' sermon and certain parts had penetrated the wall dividing him and Kayla. Just like God had strategically selected the three-hundred men to fight against the Midianites, God had strategically brought him and Kayla together. Kayla conceiving at the same time Danté joined them was also part of God's plan. They'd been trying for months, and Sam was genuinely excited, but couldn't risk showing it for fear of hurting Danté. Leave it to drama queen Kayla to misinterpret his consideration for detachment.

Kayla leaned her head to the side and began massaging her shoulder. Sam lurched forward at the simple gesture. It had been too long since they'd shared conversation or touched. His anger couldn't make him deny the fact that he missed his sweetheart. Sleeping next to her and smelling her soft scent without touching her was killing him. Conversation with Danté could only go so far. Sam missed Kayla's words of encouragement.

For the first time in days, they'd eaten dinner at the table as a family. Conversation was almost non-existent except for pleasantries, but at least they were together.

In an attempt to call a truce, Sam volunteered him and Danté for kitchen duty after Kayla had spent early morning and part of the afternoon cooking. Her demeanor didn't show any gratitude, but she did thank him before exiting the kitchen. He wondered what she would do now if he rubbed the kink out of her shoulder. Would she jerk away, or moan with pleasure like in times past? The fact that he questioned his wife's reaction to his touch disturbed him. How had they grown so far apart so fast? By the time he reached her, he still didn't have an answer to that question, but he was determined to get one.

He rested his hand on her shoulder to gain her attention. Her startled expression made his knees weak. Kayla had the most beautiful eyes, and when enlarged they were also sexy. By the time she removed the earplugs, Sam was sitting in the wicker chair beside her.

"What?" she said, resuming a relaxed position.

Neither her one-word response nor her tone was welcoming, but Sam pressed forward anyway.

"Kayla, we need to talk." He paused for her reaction, but there wasn't any. "I need to ask you something." He wanted to hold her hand, but couldn't until she answered his questions.

Kayla set the book on the table with more animation than Sam thought necessary. If the patio furniture had been glass-top, glass wedges would be flying. He could do without the loud exasperated sigh as well, but at least she made eye contact.

She looked around. "Where's Danté?"

"He's getting his clothes together for his big day tomorrow. Then he's going to take a bath. I thought this would be a good time for us to talk."

"Go ahead, you're in control."

He ignored the dig, and went straight to the point. "Kayla, did you mean what you said about me the other day? Do you really think I use you for sex and help with the bills? Do you really believe I don't care about our baby?" Sam had to stop, before the internalized anger spewed out.

Kayla folded her arms, but instead of attitude, Sam thought he saw remorse. "Of course, I didn't mean the part about sex and the bills. I was angry, and I'm still mad at you for shutting me out with that stringent plan you concocted. We're a team; at least we used to be."

Involuntarily his hand rested on hers. "I didn't shut you out. All I did was try to bring some normal order into Danté's life. Why can't you see that?"

"Why can't you see that Danté is not just your responsibility? He's ours. I promised Sherri I would love and raise Danté as my own, just like you did, but for some reason you're denying me the chance to fulfill my promise." Her lower lip trembled, and Sam knew tears weren't far behind. "I fell in love with Danté that first night we attended the play. Danté used to care about me too, but now he hates me. And you act as if you don't need me."

Sam's arm went around her shoulder, and without reservation, he pulled her to him and kissed her forehead. "Sweetheart, of course I need you. And what is this about Danté hating you?"

"He rarely addresses or speaks to me. When he does, it's to tell me how much he doesn't want or need my help. He used to hug me, but now he won't let me near him. And he hates my cooking."

Sam thought the notion was ludicrous. "Where did you get that crazy idea from? You saw him eat two heaping servings of your lasagna today."

"Well, that was a fluke, because he didn't touch anything else I'd made for him. He even wants to do his own shopping."

Sam listened, but refused to accept Kayla's interpretation as reality. He noticed Danté had been unusually quiet around Kayla, but didn't think much of it. Sherri's death was still fresh and Danté needed time to heal. Of course Danté cared about Kayla; the day she left the house angry, he'd asked about her whereabouts nonstop.

"I'm sure it's not as bad as you think," he said, trying to reassure her. "Danté is just trying to adjust. You are right about one thing: We are a team. I should have included you in my planning. Once again, I wasn't fair to you. For that, I am sorry. I'll try to do better. We'll sit down and come up with a workable plan together."

Kayla appeared to search his eyes for truth, something he'd never seen her do before. "Alright. I can pick him up from school on the days you have appointments. And—"

"We'll get to the details in a minute," Sam interrupted, "but there's more we need to discuss."

She nodded. "I'm listening."

"You accused me of not wanting our baby. You think I'm detached and ashamed of the life we created.

How could you say something like that?" Sam paused to swallow the lump forming in the back of his throat before his voice cracked. "I get that you're independent and don't necessarily need me. You may have regrets about marrying me, but to imply that I won't love my child was uncalled for. You know me better than that; at least I hope you do."

Sam held his breath, waiting for Kayla's response. Voicing his pain, made him realize just how vulnerable he was to this woman. If Kayla indeed regretted marrying him, it would mean he failed as a man.

"I do need you," Kayla admitted, placing her hand over his. "That's why I was so angry. I need you to be happy about and involved with our baby, but all you talk about is you and Danté. I waited for what seemed like forever to share this precious gift with you. I want to shout to the world that finally the manifestation of our love is on the way, but I can't because you won't let me. For the first time in our relationship, I can't share my feelings and excitement with you, because you're not interested."

"And regrets?" He had to know.

"I don't regret marrying you, but I miss our closeness. We seemed to have grown miles a part in just a few days. What's worse is I don't know how to close the gap."

The tears flowing down her cheeks gave Sam the assurance he needed. Kayla was just as miserable as he'd been. Sam lifted her from the chair and placed her on his lap. He wanted to kiss her, but now wasn't the time; unfinished business remained. If he kissed her now, he wouldn't be able to stop. For consolation, he settled for holding her snug against his body.

"Sweetheart, I miss us too. We'll figure out how to bridge the gap together. Just so you know, since the moment you told me you're pregnant on the plane, I've thanked God every day for blessing us. I pray for the health of our baby every day. I can't tell you how many times I've drifted off in a daydream about what our child will look like."

Kayla raised her head to meet his eyes. "For real?"

"For real. I can't wait to see its image or hear its heartbeat on Wednesday at your prenatal appointment."

For the first time in days, a genuine smile brightened Kayla's face. "You're coming?"

"Of course, love. You and our family are important to me. I was wrong for forcing you to keep our good news a secret. After the appointment we'll tell everyone, starting with Danté."

"Together?" she asked cautiously.

"Together. I don't want Danté to feel like we're trying to replace him, so I have to be careful with how I tell him."

"*We*, Sam. How *we* tell him," she corrected.

"How we tell him," he confirmed with finality. "I love you, woman. Don't ever think that I don't need you," he said, just before kissing her lips. When Kayla returned the kiss, Sam almost cried out with joy, but restrained himself and reluctantly broke the kiss. "Right now, I need you to help me revise a daily schedule for Danté. Tomorrow is his first day of school and I want him to be prepared."

Her giggles surprised him.

"What?"

"Pastor Sam, I love you, but you have a lot to learn about raising kids. The boy is ten years old; you can't plan every minute of his day, like he's going to daycare. Give him some space to be a kid. And please don't show up in his class unless he invites you to."

"I was only going to stay the first hour to help him get adjusted to the new school," Sam explained.

"He's a fifth-grader; he'll adjust just fine without the great Pastor Jerrod following him around."

Sam didn't know what to say, so he resorted to pouting.

"Come, on," she teased, while pinching his chin. "You remember how embarrassing it was for your mother to visit you at school."

"That's because she was bringing me lunch money in a Ziploc bag filled with coins."

"You ate, didn't you?" He nodded. "So stop knocking my coin collecting mother-in-law for making sure her baby had food."

"What does that have to do with anything?" Kayla had a way of taking the longest route between points when expressing her point of view. Sam doubted she'd find a common point between him protecting Danté and his mother's fear of wasting one penny.

"It's simple. Mama Stella showed up at that school with one goal in mind—to make sure her son had food. She was demonstrating her love and concern for you by giving you what she had. Her motive was right, and I'm sure you appreciated having some form of money to buy lunch, but the delivery embarrassed you. It's the same thing with Danté. Your motive is right, but having his six-feet-plus, pastor-dad hovering over him is going to embarrass Danté and probably earn him a nickname he'll carry throughout high school."

"But—" Sam started, but didn't finish. Kayla had made her point and it made sense. Having the right motive doesn't always yield the best actions. If that were the case, he and Kayla wouldn't have spent the past few days not speaking to one another.

"I get it," he conceded. At that moment, the three words became more than a catchy phrase to him. If he were to succeed at anything, he needed his drama queen, slow-to-the-point sweetheart, right beside him.

Chapter 11

"Ashley, my girl, I knew I could count on you. Now I owe you a vacation." Kayla had been singing Ashley's praises all day. During Kayla's absence, her assistant had run the retail store with the same precision as Kayla. The floor displays were current and sales reports were showing a five-percent increase.

Ashley's eyes lit up with mischief. "Thanks. I'll take a round-trip ticket to Hawaii, please."

Kayla looked up from the data sheets. "One ticket? Don't tell me you're going to leave Bobby Chen Li on the mainland while you chase those Polynesian men around."

If Ashley's smirk was any indication, things weren't going so well with Mr. Li.

"*Leroy*, can stay right here, in the state of confusion by himself. I'm done waiting for him to figure out who he is and who he wants."

Kayla closed the binder and gave Ashley her full attention. "Whoa. Hold on. I was only gone two weeks. What happened?"

"Nothing," Ashley answered with a shrug. "I just decided I'm not going to wait around for him to commit. If we're meant to be, we'll find our way back together. Besides, now that I've rededicated my life to Christ, I can't be chasing unsaved men around even if they're six-feet and superfine. Now that I think about it, make that a round-trip ticket to one of those Holy Land retreats. I don't want to lead myself into temptation with all those thick muscular men on the island. You know, the native men don't wear pants."

"I know and that's easy access for you. Wait," Kayla paused, as excitement bubbled in her belly, "Did you just say, you've rededicated your life to Christ?"

"Stop gaping at me." Ashley's lips smacked and her eyes rolled, but Kayla knew she wasn't offended or irritated. "Don't look so surprised. I'm a preacher's kid, eventually I was going to find my way back to the Lord. But I'm only committing to church service on Sunday and a weekly Bible Study. Those days of church seven days a week are over for me. That's why I'm joining Grace Temple and not my father's church; they have church too long. I mean, the Bible clearly states Jesus is standing at the door, knocking. All we have to do is let Him in. It shouldn't take five hours of hollering, prophesying, dancing and running around the sanctuary to let the Lord in. Why can't we just open our hearts to Him on the way to church? That way we could be in and out in less than two hours."

Giggles poured from Kayla, more from joy over her friend's rededication than over Ashley's assessment of how long worship service should last.

"I'm so happy for you!"

The bear hug from Kayla left Ashley winded. "I knew you would be. I wanted to tell you, but I didn't want to bother you while you attended to Sam and Danté," Ashley explained once her breathing settled. "The Saturday after you left, I decided I was tired of running. So, I stopped."

"I know the feeling," Kayla said, as her eyes began to water. The day she almost lost Sam and stopped running from God was still fresh in her memory.

"So how are those two handsome men doing? How is Danté adjusting?" Ashley asked the question before picking up the box of hangers and starting for the stockroom.

Kayla followed behind at a slower pace, pondering how to answer the question. After making up with Sam last night, they spent the remainder of the evening arranging their schedules to allow both of them to participate in Danté's care. They also planned a weekly menu and divided the cooking duties. They also agreed on some chores for Danté. The evening ended with Kayla falling asleep tucked under Sam's arm. Kayla was optimistic about their progress, but her intuition warned the battle was not over.

This morning when Kayla handed Danté the lunch she'd prepared, he thanked her without making eye contact, but during the brief prayer Sam prayed before leaving, he squeezed Kayla's hand. When Sam's good-bye kiss on Kayla's lips lingered, Danté groaned like most kids his age would do and went outside. Perhaps they were settling into a normal family life; Kayla wasn't sure.

"Today is Danté's first day of school. Other than having to talk Sam out of joining him in class, they're doing fine," Kayla finally answered, truthfully. Together, Sam and Danté were great.

Ashley looked up from the box she'd just dropped in the corner. "And you? How are you adjusting to full-time motherhood?"

"I'm a work in progress." Kayla wanted so much to share her pregnancy with Ashley, but she'd promised Sam she'd wait two more days. "It's amazing how different things are now that Danté is with us permanently. Being totally responsible for a child is a lot different from summer vacations and winter breaks."

"That's why I'm not sure I want any," Ashley said, shaking her head. "I can barely take care of myself."

"Well, I want a house full." Kayla made the declaration with her head held high.

Ashley smirked. "Spoken like a woman who hasn't experienced labor pains. I was in the delivery room for both of my sister's kids. After she ripped that pillow in half, I started to tell the doctor to pull, cut and burn my tubes right then and there."

"On second thought, I'll wait and see how this one goes." The words slipped out once she stopped laughing, but Ashley assumed she was referring to Danté.

"Then I guess you won't be having any more, because Danté is going to be a handful. Especially, since you and

Sam don't believe in spankings and believe everything them childless therapists write in a book. I give Danté a month before he has you and Sam in a 'timeout'."

Although Kayla didn't like Ashley making fun of her childrearing books, she laughed along with her. Kayla was used to wisecracks about her relying more on the words of licensed professionals than experienced parents. She and Sam would prove all children need is love, support and the freedom to express their opinion.

"Whatever, girl." Kayla watched Ashley's bob flounce away, while mentally reviewing the chapter she'd read last night. The book was written by a family therapist with over twenty-five years of clinical experience. Like Ashley guessed, the expert didn't have any children, but with that many years in practice and three bestselling books, the woman had to know what she was talking about.

Last night's chapter had emphasized the importance of being your child's friend. The therapist believed that like with adults, friendship was necessary to build trust with children. Trust would then lead to better communication and well-rounded children. The chapter ended with suggestions on how to build the friendship. Kayla planned to try two of the exercises after dinner.

∞

After reviewing reports, checking e-mails, returning phone calls, and going over his weekly schedule with the office secretary, Sam sat in his office dumbfounded. In anticipation of Danté's first day of school, Sam had cleared his morning schedule to accompany him to school. Even after Kayla suggested his presence would embarrass Danté, Sam planned to hang around for little while, at least the first hour, but Danté denied him the opportunity. As soon as Sam finalized the registration paperwork, the counselor whisked Danté away before Sam could remind him of where his office was, and that he was just a phone call away. Danté probably got the point during the ride to school. Sam had talked nonstop, going over emergency scenarios. "See you later, Dad." Danté had made the statement while following in a steady pace behind the counselor.

As Danté blended in with the sea of green and khaki uniforms, Sam conceded his wife had been right. Danté was not a baby, but a ten-year-old child who'd experienced more heartache than some adults twice his age. Even still, as a father, Sam didn't want to disappoint him. As a child, Sam had experienced too many broken promises from a selfish man who cared more about the latest car or gadget than the son he fathered. The deepest and longest conversation Sam remembered having with his father involved a nineteen-sixty-six Ford Mustang his father was restoring.

Sam vowed that wouldn't happen with Danté, or any of his future offspring. His children would always go to bed knowing where their father was, and know his love for them surpassed his desire for anything else.

"Welcome back to work."

Sam's head jolted upward. Pastor Simmons' baritone voice startled Sam; he hadn't seen him enter the office. "Hello, sir." Sam relaxed back in the chair.

"I didn't mean to startle you," Pastor Simmons said, while taking a seat. "I am surprised to see you working today." He snickered.

"Why is that?" Sam responded hesitantly, taking note of the snicker. "I told you on yesterday, I'd be back."

Pastor Simmons nodded, almost in slow motion. "Yes, you did say that." He paused and Sam knew a wisecrack was coming by Pastor Simmons' trademark mischievous grin. "I know that's what you said, but I'd thought you would be following Danté around, making sure he didn't get lost going from one side of the hallway to the other."

The manufactured defense lodged in Sam's throat and poured out in laughter. "You must have been talking to Kayla. I'm not that bad."

Pastor Simmons joined in the laughter. "You're right, son. You're much worse. Kayla didn't have to tell me anything; my eyes work just fine. You and that boy are inseparable, but I get it. Really, I do. You're passionate about being the good father you never had. You and Kayla are all Danté has. He needs your unconditional love and stability. As a professional psychologist, I also suggest you get him into counseling. Sessions for the three of you aren't a bad idea either."

Sam admired his spiritual leader's ability to find laughter in the most dysfunctional situations.

Pastor Simmons quickly sobered and stood to leave. "Speaking of stability," he said, just before exiting, "whatever is wrong with you and Kayla, fix it before you come to Bible Study on Wednesday. I don't want to experience another service with the two of you shooting darts at one another like I did on yesterday." Then he was gone.

Sam's jaw dropped. He wondered how Pastor Simmons knew he and Kayla had been feuding. Then he remembered Pastor Simmons' keen discernment. He flopped back in his chair and wondered how many others had seen through his "holy" act. It didn't matter, after last night's talk, he and Kayla were back on track, and Sam vowed nothing would disrupt the peace in his home.

Chapter 12

Kayla walked past the door to Danté's room three times before she conjured up enough courage to step inside. The drive home from school had been uneventful with the only conversation offered by Danté being an inquiry as to Sam's whereabouts. When Kayla explained he had to make an emergency trip to visit a sick congregant, Danté sulked and directed his attention out the window. Actually, the church member was on hospice and Sam had gone to offer final communion, but Kayla thought it best not to share the details considering Sherri's recent death. Once they arrived at home, Danté hibernated in his room. Barely thirty minutes had passed and Danté had changed clothing and was now seated at his desk, reading.

At least he changed out of his uniform, Kayla thought, observing the neatly hung tan pants and dark green sweater on the closet door. The white polo-style shirt lay in the hamper.

During what little downtime she had, Kayla reviewed the chapter on friendship-building, and had memorized some techniques. Yet with all the information and knowledge, Kayla was nervous about trying one of the recommended exercises. All she had to do was ask Danté about his day, and then share the highlights from her activities. According to the author/therapist, the exchange would show Danté that Kayla not only cared about his activities, but also that she was willing to be transparent and share her life with him. Earlier, Kayla had considered Sam's emergency call a confirmation to her plan to strengthen her fragile relationship with Danté. Now she wasn't so sure, but she stepped completely inside the room anyway.

"So, what are you doing?" The words fumbled out of Kayla's mouth, after she cleared her throat. If Danté's facial expression was any indication, the question was as stupid as it sounded. "I mean, what are you reading?"

"My reading assignment for the month," he answered, then continued reading as if Kayla wasn't standing next to him.

"I remember that book from school." Kayla sat on the edge of his bed, more at ease now that they had something in common. "Wait until you get to the coronation scene; that was too funny. And—"

"Miss Kayla," he cut her off. "I can read. I don't need your old-school summary."

Since Kayla was in the middle of a sentence when he interrupted, her mouth hung open. It remained that way until she realized Danté had resumed reading. Deflated,

Kayla mentally recited the author/therapist's philosophy on open communication.

She tried again. "So, how did you like your first day at the new school?"

"Fine."

"Did you make any friends?"

"I met some people."

Frustrated with the evasive answers, Kayla began sharing her day. "My day was good, considering it was my first day back. Ashley ran the store in my absence just as good as I would have. Some really cute stuff came in while I was gone. I have already picked out a few outfits. This lady came in and attempted to try on a size-ten skirt knowing full well she was a size sixteen. And had the nerve to get mad at me when the skirt didn't fit." Kayla's rant continued until Danté slammed the book shut and rose from the chair.

"Don't you have some friends your age to talk to?"

"Well, yes," she stammered, not certain how to respond.

"Good. Will you please go talk to them, because I don't care about women trying on clothes or cute outfits. I don't want to talk. I have homework to do."

"I was just trying to chat with you," Kayla explained. "I didn't mean to take you from your homework," she conceded her timing may have been off.

"If I wanted to chat, I'd be on the Internet," he snapped. "If I wanted to talk to you, I would have invited you in the first time you passed my door. I don't want to talk, so leave," he ordered.

Kayla's face twisted as she tried to remember the author/therapist's suggestions on how to handle the adverse situation, and could only remember one.

"Danté Thomas, I will not allow a ten-year-old child to order me around in my house. As long as my name is on the deed, I will go into any room I want to, when I want to. Why don't you take a timeout and think about what it means to respect adults?" She pointed to any empty corner.

He smirked. "*You* need a timeout for stopping me from doing my homework to talk about a woman trying on clothes." He leaned into her personal space. "I told you I don't need your help. Me and my dad can get along just fine without you."

Kayla bit her tongue to keep the pain those words inflicted from coming forth.

"Since you insist on being here, why don't you go and make dinner. What you made on yesterday was better, but you could still use more practice. I would come down and teach you, but I have homework. I promised my mother I'd do good in school."

"Well," Kayla corrected, more to deflect the emotional pain, Danté's words had caused than to teach him correct English. "You'll do well."

"I can't do good or well, if you keep running your big mouth about nothing."

Kayla felt the twitching in her neck, but was too busy folding and unfolding her arms to care. If she didn't gain control of her arms soon, she was sure a hand would land upside his head. She'd vowed never to hit Danté, but at the moment, she wanted to lay him across her lap and lay hands on his backside. Kayla wouldn't have dreamed of disrespecting her mother in that manner.

Kayla began pacing from the desk to the door, praying her temper would subside before she said or did something that would inflict more emotional pain on the wounded child. She gave up pacing after noticing Danté had put on headphones and was reading, like she wasn't even in the room.

The author/therapist hadn't presented this scenario in the book, so Kayla didn't know what to do. Not only had the exercise gone array, but the wedge between her and Danté had grown. After Danté laid the book down and began writing in his notebook, Kayla finally did what Danté suggested—she went to the kitchen and started dinner.

Chapter 13

"Baby, calm down before you fall off the table," Sam cautioned Kayla upon entering the exam room.

"I can't help it," Kayla squealed, and scooted back up the table. She couldn't contain the excitement if she wanted to. She'd waited too long for this moment. Not even the previous night's disastrous communication exercise and Danté's foul attitude at breakfast this morning could seep her joy. She rubbed her abdomen while smiling at Sam. "I'm glad you could make it," she said, squeezing his hand.

He squeezed back. "I told you I'd be here."

He had told her he'd come to her first prenatal appointment, but Kayla didn't have the heart to tell him she had doubted his promise. With Sam's preoccupation with Danté, Sam's behavior had become unpredictable.

"You did, but with Danté's behavior this morning, I thought you had changed your mind."

Danté had decided to sleep twenty minutes longer after the alarm sounded and when he should have been getting dressed, Danté played the PlayStation. When he finally came down for breakfast, it was time to leave, but Sam allowed him to take his time and eat. When Kayla left the house, Danté was chewing pancakes with only minutes to get to school. Kayla didn't know if he'd taken the lunch she'd packed for him or not.

Sam leaned into her space, but stopped short of kissing her lips. "Baby, nothing could keep me from being here with you. I can't wait to hear our baby's heartbeat."

The moment was too precious for Kayla to ruin with doubts. She stopped short of expressing her thoughts and smiled back. "Have you thought of any names?"

A soft knock on the door delayed Sam's answer. He and Kayla turned toward the door just as the doctor entered the room.

"Good morning, Mrs. Jerrod. I'm Dr. Kaur."

After a brief visual inspection, Kayla determined the woman with the long black hair and welcoming smile was friendly. She'd already read the doctor's bio on the hospital's website and patient testimonials. Dr. Kaur was well-educated and came highly recommended.

"Good morning," Kayla answered back, and accepted her extended hand. "Kayla is fine."

"And you must be Pastor Jerrod," Dr. Kaur acknowledged, while shaking Sam's hand.

Like Kayla, Sam instructed Dr. Kaur to use his first name.

Impressed that Dr. Kaur had taken the time to familiarize herself with her new patient, Kayla relaxed knowing she'd chosen the right physician. The grin on Sam's face expressed his satisfaction as well.

Dr. Kaur sat on the stool at the mini-desk and tapped the computer screen.

"Congratulations on your first baby?" she said, once facing them again.

"Thank you," Kayla and Sam responded, almost simultaneously. Kayla had gotten used to the giddiness she experienced whenever she thought of the baby growing inside her, but the nervous chuckling from Sam surprised her.

"Relax. I'm going to explain the process and then I'll answer any questions you may have. How does that sound?"

The loud sigh of relief from Sam as he plopped down in the chair next to the exam table made Kayla laugh. "Sounds like a plan to me," Kayla answered.

Kayla listened as Dr. Kaur explained the stages of pregnancy, and what to expect in each one. She went over diet and exercise, and symptoms that could indicate a problem with the pregnancy.

"Any questions or concerns?" Dr. Kaur asked after instructing Kayla to lay back on the exam table.

"Is it a boy or girl?" Sam blurted, before Kayla got into position.

Dr. Kaur laughed. "Well, Dad, I won't be able to tell you today. You'll have to wait about fourteen more weeks for that, but we can hear the heartbeat today." She then squeezed gel onto Kayla's stomach.

Kayla reached for Sam's hand, and when he accepted, pulled him closer to the exam table. His genuine excitement over their baby made her heart sing, and touching him was the only way she could express her feelings. Just before their lips met, the probe for the ultrasound machine made contact with her stomach.

Kayla's head snapped around. "What's that noise?"

Dr. Kaur explained how the high frequency sound-waves worked while moving the probe at a steady pace over Kayla's abdomen. "There you are," she said and outlined a section on the monitor. "That's your baby's heartbeat."

The strong rhythmic sound filled the room and sent tears cascading down Kayla's cheeks. She looked up at Sam. His eyes lit up brighter than normal.

"Sounds like a boy to me," Sam announced while wiping Kayla's cheeks.

"Or girl," Kayla rebutted.

"There's a fifty-fifty chance both of you are right," Dr. Kaur mused. Kayla and Sam debated the probability while Dr. Kaur completed the exam. "Your due date is July twenty-third," Dr. Kaur announced and replaced the probe on the machine.

A peaceful quiet filled the room as Kayla's thoughts fast-forwarded to the day she'd finally get to hold her baby. She determined Sam was having the same thoughts by his dazed facial expression.

"Are there any more questions for me?"

The couple shook their heads in response.

"If anything comes up, don't hesitate to call, or email me," Dr. Kaur instructed and handed both Kayla and Sam her business card.

Before Dr. Kaur cleared the threshold, Sam picked Kayla up and spun her around. When he came to a stop and Kayla protested, he silenced her with a kiss. "We're having a baby," he sang, while setting her on her feet.

"The house is empty; let's go home and celebrate," she suggested with more than a hint of mischief. "I don't have to be at the store until noon." Kayla's giggles stopped abruptly once Sam retrieved his cell phone and began dialing. Was he about to turn down spending time with her for work? She turned away and began gathering her belongings. Today was a good day. She'd just listened to her baby's heartbeat and Sam had kept his word and showed up to share in her joy. He was making an effort, and she wouldn't ruin the moment by complaining.

"Hey, Ma. I hope you're ready to be a grandmother."

Kayla's purse strap slipped from her fingers and into the chair. The goofiest expression she'd ever seen on Sam's face surprised her when he turned around. All his teeth were visible and most of his gums.

Kayla gapped at him, not knowing how to respond. Just a second ago, she'd assumed he was ready to desert her for the sake of church work, but Sam had kept his word.

"That's right; your grandson will be born on July twenty-third." Sam moved closer to Kayla and wrapped his arm around her shoulders. He moved the phone away from his ear and looked down at Kayla. "She said, she knew when she saw you in Indiana, but didn't say anything because of the circumstances. She bought a case of newborn diapers on sale last week."

Kayla bent over with laughter. Leave it to Mama Stella to celebrate the event with a sale. No doubt, the baby would have a year's supply of diapers before it's born.

After sobering somewhat, Kayla reached for Sam's cell phone. "Correction, Mama Stella. Sam meant to say granddaughter."

"Grandson or granddaughter, it doesn't make me any difference. I'm going to pray for a healthy baby and for you and Sam to stay on track."

"Please do." The words slipped out before Kayla could stop them. Hopefully, Mama Stella would miss the indication something was wrong in paradise. Sam retrieved the phone before she spilled the beans.

"Talk to you later, Ma. We have some celebrating to do." Sam reattached his cell phone and guided Kayla toward the exit. "Let's not waste any more time. We'll call your mother on the way to the parking garage." He glanced at the clock on the wall. "We only have ninety-five minutes for our private celebration."

Kayla cried silent happy tears hugged up next to Sam as they waited for the elevator. For now, the storm had ceased.

Chapter 14

"Do you think it's over the top?" Kayla asked as soon as he stepped through the door.

Sam shook his head and placed the takeout containers on the island. In just a few short hours, Kayla had transformed their kitchen table into a baby wonderland. A baby girl wonderland, that is. Pink balloons and streamers outlined the parameter. Strawberry-iced cupcakes topped pink plates and napkins and rested on a pink and white tablecloth alongside pink cups filled with pink lemonade.

Sam reached for her and pulled her to him. "Get your infatuation with pink out now, because you will not dress my son in all pink," he announced, before kissing her.

"And you're not making my daughter play football." She pinched his cheek, and then looked over his shoulder for her first baby. "Where's Danté?" She hadn't heard him come in, but he was never far behind Sam.

Sam's shoulders shrugged. "He's probably in his room changing out of his uniform. You know he hates it."

Kayla thought to mention it was rude for Danté to enter their home without speaking, but decided against it. The parenting books emphasized positive reinforcement over complaining. Besides, the day had been perfect. Although quick, Sam left her completely satisfied after their mid-morning bonding session. She couldn't risk getting into another argument over Danté and ruining the evening.

"How do you think he's going to take the news?"

Sam stepped back and reached in the cabinet for plates, after shrugging his shoulders. "For ten years, he's been an only child. I'm sure he'll welcome the responsibility of being a big brother."

Kayla opened a container and sniffed the Chinese dish, something she'd started doing lately. "Let's pray he's not overbearing and controlling like my big brother."

Sam paused from collecting serving utensils and smirked at her. "Don't act like you don't bask in Carlos' attention. He's spoiled you, and you love it."

"Maybe a little," Kayla admitted, while removing the tongs from Sam's hand. "But I love the way you—"

"What's going on?" Danté's sudden appearance ended Kayla's flirtation before it got started.

Kayla placed the box of fried rice back on the island. The parenting book may have made an oversight, but manners still mattered to Kayla. "Hello, Danté. How was school?" To her surprise, the Danté she loved made an appearance.

"School was alright. We started preparing for the science fair. I think I want to build a drone. How was your day?"

Huh? Kayla wasn't expecting a response, let alone an inquiry about her day. Momentarily, she glanced at Sam to see if he'd coached the boy. It wouldn't have mattered; no one was ruining her day. "My day was great," she said, while rubbing her stomach.

Sam cleared his throat. "Let's eat, before the food gets cold." With hands held out, he waited for his family to join hands with him.

"Okay, but what's all this icky pink stuff for?" Danté asked again.

"We're celebrating, and I'll tell you what we're celebrating between the egg rolls and the cupcakes."

Kayla nearly squealed, when after saying grace, Sam squeezed her and Danté to him and kissed their foreheads. She made a point then to stop second-guessing her place in Sam's heart. Like her, this was Sam's first time loving someone. So what if he didn't get it right all the time?

"Wow, Miss Kayla, you're hungry," Danté pointed at Kayla's plate, taking note of Kayla's larger-than-usual portions. "Did you eat today?"

Kayla appreciated the concern, but why did he still put "Miss" on her name? They were a family now, why couldn't Danté acknowledge that? *Today is a happy day,* she kept thinking until Danté repeated the question.

"Of course I did," Kayla said, before stabbing a broccoli spear. "I think my appetite is increasing." Instinctively, her free hand rubbed her stomach.

Danté's searing stare slowed Kayla's chewing. What on Earth was he thinking? Could he sense his little sister's presence?

"Son, I know you're not going to let that sesame chicken get cold, after you practically bribed me into buying the extra-large size. You're still washing my car."

Danté's countenance suddenly changed. "Sure thing, Dad." The mischievous grin returned, right before he popped a piece of sesame chicken inside his mouth.

Danté's vision for creating a master drone dominated the majority of the dinner conversation, with Sam and Kayla asking questions about the technology.

"I'm ready for my cupcake. What are we celebrating?" Danté repeated, after finishing off the last egg roll.

Kayla's chest tightened, and for once she feared Danté's response to their announcement. What if he wanted to remain an only child? She silently berated herself for not consulting one of her many parenting books. The feel of Sam's arm scooting her closer to him erased her fears. Sam was excited, and that weighed more than a temper tantrum of a ten-year-old.

"Well, son," Sam began. "Remember how I explained children are a blessing, and that all children come from God?" Danté nodded. "Well, God has blessed us by increasing our family."

Kayla's head slightly shook at her husband's approach. *Please don't give this child a theological dissertation. Just tell him he's going to be a big brother in a few months.*

"I know. That's why I'm here." Kayla snickered as Danté gave Sam one of those *duh* looks. "You didn't have to put up all this icky pink for that. A new PlayStation game would have been fine."

Sam ran his hand across his head, as if he wasn't sure of what to say next. "The icky pink stuff is not for you, although, we love having you in our family. It's time for us to grow, but don't worry, you'll always be important to us. We'll always be here for you no matter what."

"Honey, let's not scare him," Kayla interjected once Danté's eyes enlarged. "This is good news, remember?" She grabbed Sam's hand to communicate to him that maybe she should break the news to Danté.

Sam's relief was evident in the exasperated breath he let out. "You're right. Why don't you tell him?"

I don't know why it's so hard for you to say the word baby, is what Kayla wanted to say, but instead faced Dante. "How do you feel about the responsibility of—"

"A dog! We're getting a dog?" Danté interrupted. "That's great! I always wanted a dog."

"Dog?" Kayla stuttered.

"Yes," he shouted with arms in the air. Can we get a big one, like a German shepherd?"

For the first time in days, Kayla observed sheer happiness permeating from him. His eyes brightened and a full-smile filled half of his face. She looked to Sam for assistance.

It was Sam's turn to stutter. "Well, son, we're not getting a dog. You're going to be a big brother. We're having a baby."

Kayla was seated close to Sam, but couldn't hear him breathe, or feel herself breathe in the seconds that followed.

Danté's face twisted, then relaxed. "A baby?"

"Yes, a baby," Sam answered, and Kayla nodded.

"A boy or girl?"

"A boy."

"A girl." Kayla and Sam answered simultaneously, then erupted with laughter.

"Both? A brother and a sister?" Danté questioned.

"No, son. Just one, but we don't know if it's a boy or girl, yet," Sam clarified, then looked at Kayla. "We're happy with whichever God blesses us with."

Danté nodded as if he understood, then dropped a question of his own. "What does God have to do with anything? Didn't the baby happen because you have sex a lot?"

Kayla's cheeks burned, and Sam's stuttering returned.

"Sex? What do you know about sex?"

Danté smirked. "Really, Dad? I'm ten. I know how babies are made, and I know what's happening when I hear that knocking noise from your bedroom. It's the same noise my parents used to make after my father beat my mother."

Sam gasped.

Kayla's jaw hung. What Danté said next floored her.

"Maybe God does have something to do with how babies are made, because Miss Kayla, you say His name a lot when you're having sex."

If Kayla wasn't utterly embarrassed, she would have joined in with Sam's boisterous laughter. What was she supposed to say to that? The parenting book didn't suggest having the sex talk for another three years. "Well, I," she stuttered. Sam squeezed her and kissed her cheek, before facing Danté.

"God has everything to do with it. He created sex for *married* people to enjoy. For married people, sex is an expression of love." His hand rested against Kayla's stomach. "The baby is a result of the love Kayla and I have for one another." His free hand reached for Danté, to hug him. "And although you came to us differently, we love you unconditionally as our own. We're a family now, and always will be."

"I'm going to be a big brother!" Danté cheered.

The genuine smile resting on Danté face warmed Kayla to the point she had to reach out and touch her son. The goofy grin had been hiding behind pain and loss for so long, Kayla almost forgot how lovable he was. Risking rejection, Kayla squeezed him and kissed his cheek. To her delight, Danté returned the hug and didn't wipe the kiss off.

Danté pulled away. "So, when is my little brother coming?"

"In the summer," Sam answered.

"In the meantime, can we get a dog?"

Chapter 15

"Excuse me!" Kayla stopped in the middle of answering a customer's question, and ran to the bathroom for the second time that day. At ten weeks pregnant, the novelty had worn off, giving way to horrific morning sickness. The pamphlets she'd read were wrong—morning sickness wasn't limited to the mornings. Kayla had all day sickness. Ginger didn't help, neither did the Saltines and toast. Small sips and tiny bites wreaked equal havoc on her stomach. Instead of gaining weight, Kayla had lost eight pounds. Even without pregnancy, her petite frame needed every pound. She bent over the toilet and pulled her hair back just before her stomach erupted.

Aside from the hyperemesis, her life was nearly normal. At home, Sam listened to her moaning and groaning, and attempted to pray her discomfort away. He and Danté handled most of the household chores. The insults from Danté' had ceased, but that's only because, aside from a few questions about the baby, he rarely spoke with Kayla. In fact, during the bad nausea and vomiting moments Danté stayed out of sight. Then, once the storm passed, he would quietly sit next to Sam, while Sam comforted her. These days, Kayla didn't mind the silent treatment, being too fatigued to care much about anything.

"Can I bring you something? Water? Crackers? Anything to keep you from spending the day with your head stuck in the toilet."

Kayla rolled her eyes upward to see Ashley standing in the doorway. "Nothing works. I just have to deal with it until it passes."

Ashley reached into the stall, and passed her a wad of tissue. "When is that? I don't remember my sisters being sick like this. Are you sure nothing is wrong with the baby?"

Kayla wiped her mouth before responding. "Unfortunately, this is quite normal. It should pass in the next couple of weeks."

"Let me guess, you read that in a book written by a barren expert."

If Ashley wanted to make Kayla find some humor in her current state, she failed. "Why don't you go call Bobby Chen Li and get on his nerves and leave mine alone." Kayla rinsed her mouth twice before realizing Ashley hadn't given a sassy comeback. In fact, Ashley hadn't mentioned the budding relationship in weeks. When she turned around Ashley was heading out the door. Kayla caught up with her in the hallway. "Hold up, girl. What's up with you and Bobby?" she asked, grabbing her arm.

When Ashley turned around, the queasiness Kayla felt was for her friend. A trail of tears outlined Ashley's cheeks—totally out of character. "What happened?"

"Absolutely nothing," Ashley answered, without eye contact. "I haven't heard from Leroy since I suggested we stop seeing each other because we are unequally yoked."

Kayla slowly nodded. "I see."

"I thought he would stage a protest. I mean, he said he cared. But I guess not enough. He just wished me well, then walked out of the restaurant and out of my life. That was twenty-one days ago."

"I'm sorry it didn't work out. Maybe it's for the best," Kayla whispered, thinking back to when Sam ended their relationship for the same reason.

"I don't know if it's for the best, but it sure hurts like heck. I think I was falling in love with him. Oh well," Ashley added, after wiping her cheeks with the back of her hand. "I can't turn back now, and I can't compromise."

Kayla squeezed her arm for comfort. "When it's the right one, you won't have to compromise. It could be the right guy, but wrong time."

"The guy, or the time, doesn't matter. It's done. I have to move on." A manufactured smile appeared. "Do you think you can get through the rest of the day in the upright position, or do I need to take you to the doctor for fluids again?"

"What about..." Kayla decided against pressing Ashley to talk about the breakup. As much as she wanted

Ashley and Bobby to work out, she couldn't encourage a relationship that could place Ashley's new commitment at risk. "No, I'm fine," she said out loud, while inwardly praying for her friend.

"I'll be out front if you need me." Ashley turned and left before Kayla could think of something comforting to say.

Kayla wasn't fine, but managed to make it through the day, alternating between her office and the register. Occasionally, she'd work on a display until her energy level dropped. Then, she'd sit in the chair Ashley placed behind the register and surf the Internet with her phone for gender neutral nursery themes. After numerous debates, she and Sam had decided to go the old-school way and not learn the baby's sex until the birth. Even so, Kayla had a secret stash of pink layette sets tucked away in the back of the linen closet.

"Can you put the phone down long enough to help a customer?"

Recognizing the voice, Kayla responded without looking up from her phone. "You're my brother, so you don't count. What do you want, and no, you can't use my discount."

"Since you have time to surf the net, check this out."

Kayla felt Carlos' arm around her shoulder at the same time the black leather book with gold letters blocked her screen. "You bought a Bible!" Her fatigue suddenly gone, Kayla jumped to her feet and tossed the phone on the counter and returned her brother's hug. "I am so happy for you, but you know, it only works if you read it."

"You know, that's the same thing Pastor Simmons told us at the new convert class."

The serene expression resting on his face was a vast improvement from their last interaction. She pulled from his embrace and slapped his arm. "Why did I have to hear from Ma that you stopped running from the Lord? Even Sam knew before I did."

He placed the Bible on the counter and folded his arms. "Jealous you aren't the center of attention? Green doesn't look good on you. Besides, I had to hear from Ma, the good reverend knocked you up."

"Seriously? It's not my fault Ma sent out a mass text while still on the line with me. Now that you've stopped running from the Lord, you can get delivered from being a control freak."

"Whoa, mija, one step at a time," he said, raising his open palms. "I'm having a hard enough time memorizing the Lord's Prayer. Seriously, how are you feeling?" he asked after they shared a brief laugh. "Sam told me about the morning sickness."

"All day sickness," she corrected, without asking when her brother and husband talked. "It's horrible. Ma says that means it's boy. She's wrong, I know it's a girl."

"What does Danté want?"

As the words rolled off her tongue, her eyes rolled also. "Of course, he wants a little brother, but that's just too much testosterone under one roof for me."

"Exactly, how well are you adjusting to motherhood and pregnancy?"

A customer with an arm full of clearance items approaching the register prevented Kayla from answering the question. She didn't mind, because Kayla really did not know how to respond. True, she and Danté had reached a truce, but he hadn't allowed her to mother him yet. "It's coming," she answered once the customer neared the door.

"But?"

"But nothing. Everything is a work in progress." Sharing her motherhood woes with her overprotective brother wasn't something she thought wise to do. Carlos adored Danté, but she doubted he would tolerate the ten-year-old disrespecting his sister, or the rough patch she and Sam had endured. "And just how are you and Jasmine?" She thought it best to change the subject before Carlos dug in deeper.

"She's the real reason I'm here. My baby's birthday is coming up, and I want to buy her something special to wear for when I tell her how I really feel about her."

Kayla's hands flew to cover her opened mouth. Her nausea suddenly forgotten and the deflection worked. "Oh, my God! Are you going to propose?"

"Of course not, but at least now we can officially be a couple. A holy couple, I might add."

Kayla couldn't help but wrap her arms around her big brother's neck. "I'm so happy for you," she said, after a quick peck on the cheek. "And to show you how much, I'll have Jasmine looking like a fashion model in minutes." She reached for his hand, but he held up his open palms instead of allowing his shopaholic sister to drag him around the store to spend a small fortune. "What?"

"I just want you to know that I didn't completely dedicate my life to God, so I could date Jasmine. I'm more concerned about establishing a deeper relationship with Jesus."

Kayla stared at her brother in awe. God was truly in the miracle-working business. If God could soften her brother's heart, certainly he could work the same miracle on Bobby Chen Li for Ashley. He could also iron out the kinks in her household. "Come on," she said, slapping his hands away. "You can tell me all about it, while I spend your money."

Chapter 16

"Hold on, Ma, let me put in my earpiece." Normally, Kayla didn't talk on the phone while driving, but since her mother called, she couldn't wait to discuss the results of her ultrasound. The 3-D images she group texted to her family were too adorable. It was only a facial image, but it reinforced Kayla's belief she was carrying a girl. It also confirmed for Sam that a male offspring was on the way. He actually had tears in his eyes as he stared at the image. Kayla didn't care how many tears of joy her husband shed, she was carrying a girl.

"Ma, isn't she adorable?" Kayla shrieked once the earpiece was secured. "Doesn't she look just like me?"

"He or she, looks like the perfect baby with the fattest cheeks."

"Come on, Ma, you know it's a girl."

"The only thing I know is, I'm going to spoil my second grandchild to death."

"Second grandchild? Unless Carlos has a lovechild hidden somewhere, this is your first grandbaby," Kayla corrected as she crossed the intersection.

"Kayla Alicia Perez Jerrod, please don't tell me you've forgotten about Danté already."

Kayla waited until she came to a complete stop at the next light before responding. She had not forgotten about Danté. As hard as she tried to embrace Danté as her son, he had yet to be receptive. Now that the morning sickness had passed, Danté was back to ignoring her unless Sam was around. Even on days she picked him up from school, he wouldn't utter a word on the drive home, then would hibernate in his room until Sam came home.

"No, Ma, I didn't forget. It's just that Danté, well he can be difficult at times."

"And what ten-year-old isn't difficult? And what does that have to do with your love for him? Difficult children are a byproduct of motherhood. If you think he's difficult now, wait until he's a teenager."

"I know, Ma, but he's not the sweet little boy I fell in love with." Kayla sighed. "He's downright mean to me."

"Remember you made his mother a promise to love him and raise him as your own. When you made that promise, you knew he carried the scars of abuse, and now he's lost his mother."

Kayla took advantage of being able to roll her eyes without Rozelle knowing. "I get all that. That's why I've been reading books to learn how to support him. But, he just doesn't like me anymore."

"You, millennials kill me with these child-rearing techniques from people with no kids. Book sense doesn't equal common sense or maternal instinct."

Rozelle's laughter irritated Kayla, primarily because the exercises and theories she read about failed to yield fruit.

"Baby, be patient with him. Don't write him off because now you're pregnant. If anything, you should draw closer to him so he doesn't feel left out after the baby is born."

"He leaves me out all the time," was Kayla's instant comeback, but she suppressed it. "I'm trying, Ma, but it's hard sometimes," she voiced instead. "Not that I expected parenthood to be easy, but I didn't expect to feel like a stranger in my own home. He loves Sam, but hates me."

"What?"

Kayla hadn't meant to say the last sentence out loud, but maybe needed to.

"Nothing, Ma. I just wish he would give me a chance. I get tired of being rejected. I won't have to worry about that with my daughter," she added, while rubbing her stomach.

"You don't have to worry about it now. Danté adores you. He may not know how to express it, but he loves and appreciates you. Just be patient and place yourself in his shoes. You, Sam and the baby you're carrying are his world."

That was easy for her mother to say. Danté acted like an angel around her.

"I hear you, Ma. I'll work on it," she vowed pulling into the store's parking lot. She hoped she wasn't lying.

∞

The alarm on Tyrell's watch sounded. "Fifty hours, til marital bliss," he exclaimed.

Sam noted the sheer happiness radiating from Tyrell's face as they had their final tuxedo fitting before Tyrell's wedding. Similar to Sam, Tyrell had waited for God to reveal his soulmate and had abstained from pre-marital sex. Sam was honored to stand in as Best Man, and refused to damper his best friend's excitement by informing him marital bliss can be fleeting.

"An hourly countdown? Really man?"

"Really!" Tyrell affirmed, as the attendant adjusted his cuff. "I've been standing in line so long for this blessing, I might break out in a dance right at the altar like you did."

Mention of his own wedding day shenanigans made Sam laugh out loud. "What can I say? God blessed me with my heart's desire."

"So you know how I feel, then?"

Sam knew exactly how his friend felt and would give anything to get that excitement back into his marriage. He and Kayla weren't fighting anymore, but the spark they once shared had dimmed. Frequent passionate lovemaking dwindled to an occasional bland obligation. Their common interests seemed to start and end with planning for the baby. Kayla rarely interacted with

Danté and left all decision-making for his care to Sam. She didn't even comment on the new study schedule he created after Danté failed a math test. The outspoken drama queen he married had taken a hiatus.

"I sure do, man, and I'm praying for your strength." Sam chuckled and turned his attention to selecting cufflinks.

Later, Tyrell posted in the doorway of Sam's office at the church. "So, do you want to talk about it now?"

Sam looked up from his computer screen. "Talk about what?"

Tyrell closed the door, before occupying the chair. "I'm not so absorbed with the wedding that I don't know when something's troubling my boy?"

Sam loved Tyrell like a brother. He'd proven to be a real friend and had been there for Sam in his darkest hour, but Sam still felt uncomfortable exposing his concerns for his marriage. Besides, the recent change in Danté's behavior in school had him worried. Not only was the quality of his work slipping, so was his attitude. Sam sat in the back of the class to observe the disruptive behavior firsthand after the teacher voiced concern. He conveniently withheld this information from Kayla.

"Man, it's Danté."

"What's going on?"

Sam threw his hands up in resignation. "Man, I don't know. First, he didn't do well on a test. Then his teacher called to say he's saying mean things and picking fights with other students."

"Not a teenager yet and already a rebel, huh?" Tyrell laughed, but Sam failed to see the humor and remained somber. "Seriously, what does he say is the reason? Is he being bullied?"

"I wish it was that easy. In every case Danté has been the aggressor. When I question him about his behavior, he just says sorry and promises not to do it again. The other day, I banned him from all video games. I don't know what else to do."

"That doesn't sound like the Danté I know. Has Kayla tried talking to him," Tyrell asked while rubbing his chin.

Sam opened his mouth to respond, but then hesitated. How could he say Kayla's interest in Danté was practically non-existent now that she's pregnant? At first, she accused Danté of not liking her. Now, Sam doubted Kayla liked the child. To keep peace, Sam chose not to voice Kayla's selfishness. He had a better idea.

"I think I'll take him to the youth center and let Bobby pick his brain."

"That might help," Tyrell offered. "Your son and the confused youth director do have history."

"Let me give him a call." Sam didn't doubt for a second Tyrell caught the deflection, but appreciated him for not pressing. Before Sam could find the number in his cell phone, the office manager knocked, then barged into his office.

"Pastor Jerrod, they need you at the school. Now! It's your son!"

Chapter 17

Kayla jumped at the sound of the garage door opening. Sam and Danté had made it home, causing her nerves to go into overdrive. She decided to take her mother's advice and make an attempt to chisel at the wall that had settled between her and Danté. Even from a distance, she sensed a change in the child's behavior. He'd stopped cleaning his room without being told. He barely finished his dinner, and she'd overheard him snap at Sam over his schoolwork. Sam had reverted back to his one-man show routine and didn't discuss the changes with her, but her intuition told her something deep was bothering Danté. She had an idea what could be the cause of Danté's deportment, but the good reverend didn't ask her opinion.

Taco Tuesday was the theme of tonight's meal. Danté loved tacos, and was sure to eat a healthy serving, or so she hoped. She made them just the way he liked them, and for dessert, homemade chocolate chip cookies. She decorated the table with taco-themed placemats and plates and taco-shaped cups, hoping to create a festive mood.

"Lord, please help me communicate with my son." She whispered the prayer just as her men walked into the kitchen through the connecting door from the garage. She hadn't expected enthusiasm, but the somber expression Sam wore was unexpected.

"Hi." Her husband greeted her with a lifeless peck on the cheek, then brushed past her. Danté followed behind with his head down without speaking.

"Dinner will be ready in five minutes. It's Taco Tuesday on Wednesday," Kayla announced to their retreating backs.

Neither Sam nor Danté acknowledged the announcement, but both were seated at the table on time. She pasted on a smile and pressed forward, determined to bridge the gap between she and Danté.

"How was your day, babe?"

Sam grunted. "Interesting."

"Danté, why are you wearing shades at the dinner table?" she asked, while placing a tray of toppings on the table. "Are you so cool you have to wear sunglasses at night now?" She giggled slightly in an attempt not to come across as fussing.

Instead of answering, Danté kept his head down.

Kayla looked at Sam for assistance.

"It's all good. He's cool."

Sam's manufactured response told her everything was not all good. They were hiding something from her and she was about to find out what.

"Don't!" Danté protested as Kayla removed the shades.

She gasped. "What happened to your eye?" The glasses fell from Kayla's hand and she stared pacing. She was not expecting to find a black ring around his swollen eye. "Who hit you?"

Sam cleared his throat. "He got into a little altercation with a kid at school today."

"Little?" She stopped pacing and glared at Sam, but pointed at Danté. "Look at his face. Who beat him up? What kind of school are they running at that church? I didn't send my child to school to be a punching bag." She stood over Danté and cupped his face. "Are you okay? Does it hurt?" Before he could answer, Kayla was pacing again. "This doesn't make any sense. Them people don' lost their mind if they think they can just let somebody beat up on my baby. I will slap some sense into every last one of them bad kids and the teachers. I'm not about to have no one bullying my child while they sit back and watch. That is a Christian school and they let this happen? I'm not about to have this. I'm taking him to school tomorrow."

Sam interrupted her rant. "Actually, Danté is the bully."

"I don't know who them people think—" Kayla stopped mid-sentence. "What did you say?"

"Before you go to the school and slap everybody, you should know in this case Danté was the aggressor, and his face looks a lot better than the other kid's."

Kayla mouth was still open, but this time no words flowed as her head bobbed from Sam to Danté. Sam was too calm.

She walked over to her husband and stared directly in his eyes. "Why aren't you bothered by this? How do you know he's a bully?"

"I, well, he," Sam stuttered.

"This is not the first time, is it?"

The longer it took Sam to answer, the more the hurt intensified. She'd gotten used to Danté shutting her out, but now her husband had left her on the outside looking in again when it came to Danté. She wondered what else she didn't know about, then wondered if she should even care anymore.

"No, it's not," Sam finally responded, looking away. "He's been having behavioral problems for a while now."

"I see. And you weren't going to tell me." Kayla swallowed the lump in her throat. She was no longer hungry, no longer excited, and no longer wanted to be in their presence. She couldn't expect Danté to open up to her, if Sam wouldn't. She pasted on an even bigger smile, determined not to let Sam see how much his actions had hurt her.

"Well," she nodded at Danté, "at least you're okay. Enjoy your dinner." She didn't have any words for Pastor Jerrod.

On the trek to her bedroom it all seemed foreign to her: the walls, the pictures, the carpet even the smell permeating from the plug-in air freshener. How did festive Taco Tuesday turn into heartbreak in a matter of minutes? Her life had a way of manufacturing its own drama moments without any help from her. The only thing that kept her from breaking down was the comfort she received from rubbing her budding belly bump. Her unborn child was the one person that needed her.

Mechanically, she discarded her work clothes and climbed into the shower. Only after the water hit her face did she let the tears flow, but she didn't cry long, just long enough to get the sting of the hurt out of her system. While drying off, she noted it was time for maternity clothes, or at least larger-sized clothing. The perfect excuse to treat herself to another online shopping spree. Her virtual shopping cart was loaded when Sam finally stepped inside their bedroom with Danté.

"Dinner was great, Miss Kayla, especially the cookies."

"Yeah, sweetheart, your tacos are the best," Sam added.

Kayla's first thought was to ignore both of them, but she remembered she was an adult and focused her attention on Danté. "You're welcome. I hope you got full."

He rubbed his stomach. "I did."

Kayla wasn't fooled by his smile, or gratitude. Danté may have enjoyed her food, but his actions when Sam was not around revealed his true feelings. Kayla held a fake smile in the awkward silence that followed.

"You have about an hour to work on homework and bathe," Sam said, looking at his watch. "And no video games."

Danté hung his head. "Yes, Dad. Goodnight, Miss Kayla," he added before leaving the room.

Kayla shook her head at the mediocre acting and turned her attention back to the computer screen in search of a discount coupon.

Sam let out an exasperated breath and plopped down on his side of their bed with his back to her. "I don't know what's going on inside that boy's head."

Kayla didn't look up. *I know he's not going to sit here and act like we're all good?*

"I got called every day last week about his behavior, and now he's fighting. If I wasn't on staff at the church, I'm sure he would have been expelled. Hopefully, the suspension will cool him off."

Kayla kept surfing. *Good thing he has the great Pastor Jerrod for a dad.*

"I sat in his class and saw and heard him firsthand disrespect his teacher and other students. It's like all of sudden Aaron Thomas' DNA has taken over."

Kayla gawked at him, but only momentarily. *So now you're blaming his abusive father whom he hasn't seen in years?*

"I've got to find out what's going on inside that boy's head, before he gets completely out of hand."

"Got it!" Kayla exclaimed.

Sam jolted around to face her. "You get why he's acting out?"

"Huh? Oh, actually, I was referring to the forty-percent off coupon I just found."

"Were you paying any attention to me?"

Kayla entered the discount code before responding to him. "I heard you." She ignored Sam's stare and finished placing her order.

"I'm glad you can shop, while our son is experiencing a behavior crisis."

No, he didn't just say that! Kayla rolled her eyes and closed the computer. It amazed her how clueless her husband was.

"Pastor Jerrod, you don't really want my opinion or assistance. If you did, you would have included me from the beginning."

Sam folded his arms, but didn't verbally disagree.

"Someday you may get a clue. Until then, I'll help you out. I noticed a change in Danté's behavior two weeks ago. His eating habits have changed and he appears to be depressed. This Sunday is Mother's Day. I'm sure he's seen countless commercials reminding him that his mother is no longer here. I'm willing to bet there has been mention of Mother's Day at school as well, maybe even a special project to commemorate the day. It's his first Mother's Day without her, and Sherri's birthday is also next week."

Sam's brow furrowed.

"In that great parental mind of yours, did it ever occur to you that Danté is acting out from the pain of not being able to have his mother on Mother's Day for the first time, or celebrate her birthday like the rest of the kids?" She shrugged her shoulders. "It's just a thought? But what do I know? You're Superdad."

Kayla reached over and turned off the lamp on the nightstand, communicating to Sam the conversation was over.

Chapter 18

S am stood in the doorway of Danté's room like he'd done every day since Danté officially became his son. Only this morning, he saw what his ambition had previously prevented him from recognizing. Unlike most kids, Danté liked his surroundings neat and in order. His clothes were always on hangers or inside drawers. His shoes paired neatly in the closet and, books neatly on his desk. His bed was always made. Sam attributed the tidiness to Danté attempting to control his environment after his chaotic beginning. Today, Danté's room looked like a war zone. Patches of carpet were barely visible underneath dirty clothes. The fitted bed sheet hugged only half of the mattress, and shoes appeared to have been randomly thrown around the room. And yet, Danté lay comfortable on the bed in the middle of the chaos, staring at the ceiling.

Kayla was right. Danté was depressed. What irked him more than admitting his wife was right, was the fact that with all of his efforts to be a good father, he had missed the signs. While making preparations to celebrate his own mother, the thought of Danté's void never crossed his mind. All he could focus on was keeping him on a schedule and making sure Danté knew he could always count on him to be there for him, regardless of the behavior.

Sure, he could have shared the change in Danté with Kayla, but he thought he had everything under control. Besides, Kayla didn't seem interested. *How did she know what the problem was?* He'd pondered that question all night while tossing and turning next to his wife, to no avail. Could he have been wrong about her disinterest in their son? The hurt she displayed, although quietly, indicated he'd misjudged her actions. He cared, but couldn't deal with her feelings right now. Danté needed him.

Sam stepped completely inside of the bedroom and sat on the bed. Momentarily, Sam observed the physical changes. The six-year-old snaggletooth kid he'd met four years ago had matured way beyond his ten years. So much trauma had plagued his young life—physical and verbal abuse by his father and the death of his mother, yet he remained focused until now.

"Hey, son."

"Hey."

Sam noticed the tears pooling at the corners of his eyes. "Want to talk about it?"

Danté shook his head from side to side. "No. I'll clean up my room today." He turned on his side.

Sam touched his shoulder. "Cleaning up this room would be great, but I was referring to your mother. You've been missing her a lot lately, huh?"

"Yes."

"Is that the reason, you've been a bully lately?"

Danté turned on his side and leaned against Sam and his dad stroked his nodding head. "I know my mother wouldn't be happy with my behavior, but I'm mad. Her birthday is coming, and I can't make her the yellow cake with chocolate icing she liked."

Sam's strokes moved from Danté's head to his little back, but he remained silent.

"I heard you on the phone ordering flowers for Grandma Stella. I want to get my mother flowers too, but I can't."

Sam laid down on the bed and held his son. The scriptures in his comfort repertoire seemed far from adequate for the sobs pouring from Danté's broken heart.

"I wish I could take your pain away, but I can't. All I can tell you is, your mother will always be with you in spirit from heaven."

"But I don't want her in heaven! I want her with me!" Danté wailed.

"I know, son. I know." Sam squeezed him tighter, totally lost for words.

∞

"He could have kept that." Kayla smirked, then tossed the Mother's Day card Sam had left on her nightstand into the drawer. She wasn't his mama. He'd probably only given her the card as a peace offering for erasing her out of his and Danté's world, again. Sam had spent the past seventy-two hours comforting Danté by showering him with attention. Father and son were practically joined at the hip, which left little-to-no room for the lady of the house. Sam was so absorbed with comforting Danté, he abandoned the warm king-sized bed he shared with Kayla and crammed his long body next to his son on a twin mattress last night. Oddly enough, Kayla didn't miss her husband's presence. Something changed in her spirit after Sam's latest stunt, but she couldn't identify what. Nor did she care to. Thinking Sam wouldn't share, Kayla had eavesdropped on him and Danté from the hallway. Her heart broke hearing Danté's pleas for his mother, and she had to find a way to soothe his pain. After exchanging her church attire for a sundress that rested snuggly around her twenty-four-week pregnant belly, she set out on a mission to make Danté's first Mother's Day without his mother less painful.

Earlier during worship service, the emotional gap that resided between Pastor Jerrod and Kayla disappeared as they both directed their attention to Danté. Instead of sending Danté to the youth service, Sam thought it best to keep Danté next to him on the front row. He hadn't asked her opinion, but Kayla agreed, and along with Sam, comforted Danté throughout most of the service. She and Sam had driven separate cars to church, which allowed her to tip out after prayer service and rush to the grocery and party stores and make it home in time to do the prep work in her quest to brighten Danté's day.

After removing the ingredients from the grocery bags and refrigerator and organizing them on the counter, Kayla retrieved the keepsake box Sherri had left for Danté from the curio. Mixed with mementos and photos, the box contained letters Sherri wrote for future events she would miss. Kayla thought looking at photos of happier times while Sherri's favorite cake baked in the oven, would be therapeutic. Then from the backyard, they would release balloons in Sherri's favorite color into the sky to honor her memory.

Where are they? she wondered, when father and son hadn't returned home thirty minutes later. After the call to Sam's phone went straight to voicemail, she began pacing. An hour and three voicemails later, Kayla was nearly panicked. She called his office at the church, no answer. Forgetting Tyrell was on his honeymoon, Kayla dialed his number and got his voicemail also. Just before she surrendered to fear and called the police, she heard the garage open. As she rushed into the kitchen, she wasn't sure if worry or anger filled her more.

"What took you so long?" tumbled from her mouth the second Sam cleared the entrance way from the garage into the kitchen. Sam avoided eye contact while hanging his keys. Instantly, Kayla knew she wouldn't like his answer.

"We went out for pizza and then to the bakery." Sam walked past her and tossed a to-go box on the counter next to her. "We brought you something back."

Kayla's heart sank as she watched a smiling Danté march into the kitchen, carrying a clear plastic food container containing a slice of yellow cake with chocolate icing.

"Hi, Miss Kayla." He looked at the kitchen table. "Are you making a cake?"

Danté had to ask the question twice before Kayla was able to formulate an answer that didn't include yelling and screaming, or worse, cursing.

"I thought we would make one together, but I didn't know you guys were going out," she answered, while shooting daggers at Sam. He brushed past her, out of the kitchen. She was still staring at his retreating back when Danté's words cut her to the core.

"I would tell you happy Mother's Day, but you're not a mother yet. You have to wait until next year."

The smirk that accompanied the declaration didn't surprise Kayla, but it did confirm Danté would never view her as anything more than Sam's wife.

"You're right." Kayla turned away and mechanically started clearing the table. Danté trotted off to his room, smiling.

When she finally entered their bedroom, Sam had changed from his suit into shorts. His bare chest revealed the scar from the wound that nearly took his life. That day, she didn't want to live without Sam. Today, she didn't want to live with Sam. She sat at the foot of the bed, debating if he was even worth conversation. "You could have told me you weren't coming straight home from service," she said after his torso was covered with a tank top.

"You shouldn't have left before service was over."

Kayla rubbed her abdomen in an effort to maintain her calm. "So, it's my fault you and Danté had dinner without me on Mother's Day? Is it also my fault you didn't tell me about Danté's behavior at school?"

Sam finished hanging his suit before responding. "If you'd shown some interest in him lately, I would have told you."

Kayla shook her head as if to clear it. "What? So, it's my fault you've shut me out of Danté's life?"

"I didn't shut you out, you alienated yourself." He sat on his side of the bed, buckling his sandals. "Sweetheart, it's been a good day. Service was good, and Danté seems to be handling today well. Can we at least wait until tomorrow to argue?"

"No." Kayla shook her head violently, while rising to her feet. "I don't think so. Your day may have been perfect, but my day has taken a turn for the worst, thanks to you. No, we're definitely going to argue today."

"Kayla, not now."

Sam's firm tone surprised her, but she would not back down. "If not now, when is it a good time to point out, once again, that you and Danté have created a world that doesn't include me?"

"You really want to do this now? Fine." Sam stood, but clear of her personal space. "The reason I didn't tell you about Danté's behavior is because the only person you seem to be concerned about is the baby?"

Kayla threw her hands up. "What are you talking about?"

"You're so absorbed with the baby; it's all you talk about. That's your only priority. Not me, and not Danté."

Almost involuntarily, the pacing began. "I can't believe you have the gall to stand here and whine about me being excited about having a baby. *Your* baby, I might add. You and Dante are always my priority, even though you act like I don't exist."

"Stop acting like you're the victim here." Sam paused, and lowered his voice. "The only time you spend with Danté is at the dinner table. Outside of that, you're not interested. You only talk to me as a courtesy. Five percent of that is about household issues, and the rest is about the baby. Honestly, we've become more like roommates who eat dinner together and have sex on occasion between baby talk and online shopping sprees."

With fists planted at her waist, Kayla yelled, "I can't believe you're jealous of your own child! If you'd show some interest in me, I wouldn't have to find comfort in our unborn child!" She lowered her voice, not wanting Danté to hear. "If I wasn't paying attention to Danté how come I knew the real reason he's acting out?"

For an answer, he turned away.

Kayla stomped around him and pointed at him. "The reason I left church early was so I could pick up everything I needed to make today more tolerable for him. I heard what he said about wanting to make a cake for his mother. I had planned to help him do that. I even got balloons he could release in her memory. So, despite what you think, I do love Danté, even though he doesn't care for me."

"Will you stop saying that!"

"It's the truth!" she roared back. "He barely speaks to me when you're not around. In his eyes, he only has one parent, and that's you. I'm someone he tolerates. So, don't blame me for being excited about having a baby of my own."

"I can't believe how selfish you are."

His piercing eyes didn't stop her from snapping back, "I can't believe how stupid you are for letting a ten-year-old control you."

"So, I'm stupid for keeping the promise I made to Sherri?"

"What about the promise you made to me to forsake all others, to always put me first?"

The longer Sam stared, the more her cheeks burned. She hadn't meant to sound like a spoiled brat, but he should not have called her selfish for wanting his attention and Danté's acceptance.

"You're just going to stand there and say nothing just like you do when there's a problem with *our* son. Well, at least you're consistent."

"Since I don't use profanity, I won't say what you've consistently been lately." With that Pastor Jerrod left the room.

Shocked at the insinuation, Kayla stayed glued in place until she jumped at the sound of the front door slamming.

Chapter 19

Attempting to make up for taking the morning off, Sam spent what normally would have been his lunch hour, pouring over the church's summer outreach plans. Number one on Grace Temple's mission statement was to meet both the spiritual and physical needs of the community it served. The Free Lunch Program, Vacation Bible School, Summer Camp, and the Back to School Supplies Giveaway, would fulfill the mission for the most vulnerable in the community. Thanks to his upbringing, he was gifted at organizing in the most economical way. In his five-year tenure as Administrative Pastor, not one of the projects he oversaw went over budget. This year his desire to plan early was intensified with Kayla's mid-summer due date.

Kayla. He shook his head. No matter how deep he delved into work, thoughts of his dysfunctional marriage always penetrated and took over his mind. Avoiding her and sleeping in the den for two nights wasn't the salve to promote healing of the wounds from their latest fight, but he wasn't ready to deal with her selfishness. His willingness to harbor animosity toward her for this long concerned him, but not enough for him to make amends. If nothing else, he had his pride and Kayla needed to grow up.

For the sake of his child, Sam suppressed his emotions and attended Kayla's prenatal appointment this morning. He'd sat on the opposite side of the waiting room, hidden behind a column, until she was called back to the exam room to see the doctor, then hurriedly joined her. He ignored the genuine shock on Kayla's face at his sudden appearance by gesturing for her to follow the nurse. During the exam, he remained by Kayla's side, but not touching her, totally engrossed in the ultrasonic heartbeat and previous lab test results. He learned Kayla's weight gain was on target and they needed to sign up for the labor and delivery tour. They also needed to get on the list for Lamaze classes soon. After expressing his gratitude to Dr. Kaur, Sam waited for Kayla to schedule the next appointment, then he left. His conscience nagged him all the way to the church, but he wasn't ready to apologize. Kayla's face infiltrated every attempt he made to pray. He knew what the scriptures said about prayers being hindered, but Sam was in no hurry to reconcile with Kayla, not the way she was now.

He turned away from the computer screen and focused on the framed photo from their first anniversary getaway on his desk and wondered if they would experience that level of happiness again.

"I didn't think you'd be in today." Pastor Simmons made the statement from the threshold.

Sam quickly focused on his mentor and boss. "Greetings, Pastor. Is there something I can help you with?"

"No, I'm fine. Just surprised seeing you here today with Kayla's appointment. That 3-D ultrasound had your mind twisted for a week."

Sam shrugged off the jesting. "I need to get a jump on summer outreach. Kayla and the baby are fine. It's Danté I'm concerned about."

Pastor Simmons stepped completely inside the office. "I heard about the boxing match. What does his therapist recommend?"

"We haven't tried therapy yet, but I've tried all of the suggestions in the books. Nothing has worked so far. I'm hoping our talk this weekend did the trick."

"So, you and Kayla are still soaking up the advice of some of my childless colleagues who wrote books. I'm sure they have some good advice, but sometimes face-to-face therapy is warranted. I could recommend a good family therapist who is also a Christ-follower, if you like? Or, I can have some sessions with him."

Sam shifted positions. Pastor Simmons concern was genuine and as a psychologist, the suggestion made sense, but Sam wasn't ready to receive it. "That won't be necessary; I think I have it under control now. Mother's Day was really tough on him, that's all." Sam stated it like he had identified the problem without Kayla pointing it out to him.

"I see."

Sam noted the contemplation veiling Pastor Simmons face and prepared to fend off another offer of help, but didn't get one.

Pastor Simmons simply nodded and said, "Since you have fatherhood all figured out, I'll continue praying for the best." Then he left.

Sam stared at the now-empty space wondering if he'd just been insulted.

∞

"Hey, daughter. You're not lost, are you?"

Kayla jumped around at the sound of Pastor Simmons jubilant voice. She'd been pacing in the vestibule and debating on if she should make the next move to bridge the gulf that separated her and Sam. His words and actions still stung, but he'd made the first step by showing up at the prenatal appointment. The fact that he remembered demonstrated he cared, but he could have spoken to her. The coldness his eyes carried wasn't inviting, but they couldn't continue like this. They also couldn't continue the way they were. Sam needed to learn how to communicate and include her in raising Danté.

Her face parted into a restful smile at the sight of the man, who led her out of the pit that had once been her life, and walked into his open arms.

"Hey, Pastor Dad." Kayla loved hugging Pastor Simmons. She imagined his hug felt like what a hug from her deceased father would feel like. Warm and secure.

"You're glowing and growing," he teased, after releasing her.

Kayla rubbed her abdomen. "She's coming along just fine."

"She?"

"Yes, sir. I'm professing and confessing her into existence."

"Aside from the pregnancy, how are you coming along?"

Just like that her smile vanished. Pastor Simmons' eyes demanded truth, besides Kayla could never lie to him. She looked over his shoulder and down the opposite hall. "Can we talk in your office?"

He nodded. "Sure."

Kayla quickly followed him down the hallway leading to his office, praying the whole time for the right way to tell Pastor Simmons how miserable her life had become. She did not want to come across as whining or jealous, but Pastor Simmons was the safest person to vent to. He wouldn't take sides and would tell her the truth. No sooner had he closed the office door, Kayla plopped down on the sofa and poured out her discontentment. His knowing expression surprised her.

In the silence that followed, he leaned back in his chair, making a teepee with his hands. "I wish you and Sam had taken my advice and had family counseling instead of depending on books and opinions. With your family dynamics, face-to-face counseling would have been more beneficial."

Kayla pouted. "You're probably right, but what can we do now?"

"For starters, you can stop calling your husband stupid."

Kayla opened her mouth to defend her actions, but Pastor Simmons cut her off.

"Daughter, even if his actions are stupid in your opinion, insulting him will only make matters worse. He's not your brother or your homie. He's your husband, and he deserves a level of respect. We men need our pride, even when we're wrong, or else we have nothing. If we feel like we're going to be attacked or rejected, we won't open up."

Kayla folded her arms and sloughed back against the pillow. "But he doesn't know what he's doing with Danté and he won't listen to me."

"Sam has never been a father before, so he's learning as he goes. He was reared by a single mother, so he doesn't have an example of how a two-parent home functions. Factor in Danté's traumatic experiences and you have the ingredients for a perfect storm. The last time I checked, this is your first time at parenthood as well. You were also reared by a single parent. Both of you are getting on-the-job training."

"I get that, but why does he shut me out?" Her voice broke along with the dam holding back her tears. "Why can't we be the team we were before? When I was the center of his attention."

His voice softened. "Daughter, you are still a team, you guys just need to establish new rules of engagement. I know beyond a shadow of a doubt that Sam loves you. From day one, he gave you his heart. The exclusion you're feeling is real, but it's not intentional. I don't believe for one second, Sam means to hurt you. You and Danté, and now the seed in your womb are his world. It may not feel like it now, but his world doesn't exist without you."

"How can you be so sure about that?" Kayla stopped her eyes from rolling in the nick of time.

"This conversation confirms the turmoil, I discerned in his spirit. He's just as miserable as you are. And just as stubborn," he added, with a smile. "You guys are going to be fine, but it's going to take time and work. Patience and love that covers a multitude of faults, not to mention prayer and counseling."

Sam didn't appear miserable while ignoring her for two days. His joy was evident at the doctor's office. He still didn't believe her when it came to Danté's attitude. Maybe they did need counseling. Like Pastor Simmons said, they both were learning how to be parents.

"Maybe we should try counseling," she conceded. "I just miss our closeness. If he ever speaks to me again, I'll talk to him about it."

Pastor Simmons chuckled. "Daughter, what you miss is, being the center of attention. I'm sure you have a way to make him talk. If not, I'll have my wife give you a call."

Kayla joined his laughter, while wondering if Sam was worth the effort.

Later at home, while gathering clothes for the cleaners, she decided her husband deserved some mercy. It was the little children's store bag containing the pink fur booties, tucked inside of Sam's suit jacket that decided it for her. The booties were cuter than the ones she had selected on her Amazon baby registry. Instead of stuffing them back into the bag, Kayla placed the dainty treasures on her nightstand and logged into her Amazon account. What should have taken a minute to update the registry, evolved into a mini-shopping spree. Too late for a run to the cleaners, she opted for a shower instead.

Her favorite scent and steam relaxed her, but the path to make amends with her husband was still blurred. Maybe break the ice by thanking him for the booties and for coming to the appointment. That seemed bland. Maybe there was some truth to his assessment of them being roommates, she pondered while lotioning her body. That saddened her.

"Hi."

Sam's monotone startled her. Inside the shower, she had not heard the alarm chime alerting her someone had entered the house. She whirled around, her towel falling in the process, and found him leaning against the doorframe dividing the sleeping area from the bathroom with his arms folded. She had no idea how long he had been standing there watching her, and wouldn't ask at the risk of starting another argument.

"I'm sorry. I shouldn't have called you stupid."

He didn't budge.

"Thank you for coming to the appointment today."

Anticipation grew with each step he took toward her, but she was disappointed when Sam stooped and retrieved the towel and held it out to her. She didn't accept it.

"Don't insult me by thanking me for being there for my child." His eyes rested on her stomach. "You're really growing. Does it move?"

"Sometimes I feel flutters. I wasn't trying to insult you."

"I know you were just being you."

When he hung the towel on the rack, his eyes revealed something she'd never seen before. She was his wife, yet he stood there wanting to touch her, but too fearful to do so. Had she bruised his ego that much? Pastor Simmons was right about one thing, she knew how to crack his shell.

She ended his turmoil by taking his hand, and after squeezing lotion into it, guided his palm onto her stomach. He didn't resist. Once he was done, she turned around and offered her back. She heard the acceleration in his breathing at the precise moment the warmth of his hands began massaging the scented fragrance into her skin.

"I like the booties." Kayla practically moaned the words, once his hands moved to her shoulders.

"I figured you would. This doesn't mean I've stopped believing it's a boy. I just thought they were cute." He gloved her abdomen from behind. "I should have told you about Danté's behavior," he said, with his chin resting against the top of her head. "And I was wrong for indirectly calling you out of your name."

Instead of voicing acceptance of what she considered a lackluster apology, Kayla let it go and moved forward. "Is the boycott of our bed over?" She faced him to see if the fear she saw earlier remained. Fear was gone, but the smoldering desire was just as unnerving.

"I was wrong for that, too. Avoidance is no way to deal with conflict."

Kayla stepped backward from the embrace and reached for a tank dress. "Just don't let it happen again."

He nodded with his eyes never leaving her stomach.

With his assistance, she smoothed the dress over her expanded midsection. "I'm going to check on *our* son." She forced eye contact by cupping his face. "At some point, we're going to have to stop being roommates and go back to being husband and wife." She stretched upward and kissed his lips. "I'm not selfish, I just miss us."

Sam's jaw fell, but he didn't voice his thoughts. His facial expression conveyed a resolution was far from fruition, but at least now they were speaking.

She found Danté perched on the couch with the game controller in his hand. First inclination was to leave him in his virtual world, but there was validity to Sam's complaint of her not spending time with the ten-year-old. She'd also made a promise to Sherri that she planned on keeping.

"How was your day at school?" she asked, after taking a deep breath.

He paused momentarily from the game and leaned around her, like he was trying to see if someone was behind her.

"Fine."

"Need some help with homework?"

"If I do, I'll ask my dad."

She stood there long after his dismissal to watch his car cross the finish line, then congratulated him on reaching the next level. Today, she'd gotten eight words out of him. Maybe tomorrow she'd get ten.

Chapter 20

"**M**an, are you reading the Bible?" Sam walked into Bobby Chen Li's office at the youth center seeking advice, but instead found more confusion. If Bobby was reading the Bible either he was in major trouble, or something traumatic occurred. "What happened?" Sam asked, after plopping in a chair.

Bobby Chen Li quickly closed the book and sat upright, looking guilty. "I'm good, just checking the good book out."

"So why do you look so lost? Is there something I can help you with?" He'd been witnessing to Bobby Chen Li for years, without much success. If there was a chance Bobby's heart was open, Sam's problems could wait.

Bobby leaned back in the chair, making a teepee with his fingers. "It's Ashley, man."

Sam started to tell him male and female relationships weren't his specialty, at least not at the moment, but his friend looked perplexed. "When did you guys get back together?"

"Humph, we didn't." Bobby Chen Li shook his head. "But that hasn't stopped me from thinking about her nearly every day since she sent me packing. I can't figure her out."

"I sure hope you're not searching the Bible in hopes of gaining an understanding of how women think." Sam chuckled.

"Man, I'm serious. We casually dated for over a year and not once did my nontraditional spiritual beliefs bother her. Then out of the blue, she starts going to church and all of a sudden everything about me is wrong and sinful."

"You had to see this coming, considering her father is a pastor and you're the grandson of a head deacon. I know you remember the story of the prodigal son in Sunday school at the Baptist church you grew up in." Sam purposefully paused in hopes of getting Bobby Chen Li to remember the spiritual foundation he insisted on running from. "Everything about you is not wrong. She just wants to live pleasing to God, and having a boyfriend who believes in a plethora of gods doesn't fit into the equation. It's not easy for her, trust me, I know."

Bobbi Chen Li shook his head as if to clear it. "Why can't she accept me the way I am? I would never ask her to change her beliefs to mine. The entire time we dated, I never attempted to convert her. Even after she set boundaries around physical activity, I still kept seeing her."

Sam resigned to the fact that no matter how he phrased the words, the truth would still hurt. "You didn't try to change her because you know she's right." Sam ignored the bewilderment on his face. "Be honest, your infatuation with every religion known to man is a form of rebellion. No matter how much you chant and change your diet, at the end of the day, in your heart you know Jesus is the only way. That's why in times of trouble you pray in the name of Jesus and quote scripture. Your spirit believes, but your flesh doesn't want to submit. You have not forgotten your foundation, but pride and stubbornness are holding you back."

Bobby Chen Li shifted in the chair. If Sam's assessment was correct, he wasn't going to give confirmation. "What brings you down here on your day off?"

"Moving right along, are we? No pressure from me, just give it some thought." Sam crossed his legs in the figure-four position. "I was wondering if you could offer some insight into Danté's latest behavioral problems." The bullying had stopped, but Danté's nasty attitude toward teachers and students remained.

Bobby Chen Li pushed the Bible away. "This I can handle. What's going on?"

Sam relayed the highlights of Danté's shenanigans, all the while feeling like a failure. He should be able to handle any parental situation without seeking help from others.

"Sounds to me like he's misplacing grief on his classmates. Is he acting out at home?"

"At home, he's perfect." He'd seen no evidence of Danté's disrespect at home, so Sam didn't find it necessary to mention Kayla's complaints.

"He still has the emotional scars from his father's violence. He might think it's normal to bully people. Maybe you should get him some counseling so he can learn ways to cope with his pain?"

Sam uncrossed his legs and stood up. Bobby Chen Li sounded like Pastor Simmons, and Sam didn't want to hear talk of counseling. Danté wasn't mentally disturbed and Sam had it under control. "Now that I've got him to admit his pain, I think he'll be okay." He pointed at the Bible. "Just in case you're free on Wednesday nights, this month we're studying the book of Acts in Bible Study. I'm sure Ashley will save you a seat," Sam teased.

"Now look who's avoiding the issue," Bobby Chen Li said, following Sam into the hallway.

"I hear you, man. I'll think about what you said." Sam inwardly repented, knowing between work, Danté and his selfish hormonal wife, there would no time to put much thought into something he found unnecessary. He continued down the hall and into the main lobby. If he hurried, he could make a surprise trip to Emery Bay and pacify his wife with undivided attention.

He and Kayla had called a truce, but their insipid relationship was more obligatory than passionate. They slept in the same bed and conversed about more than the baby, and Kayla had reinserted herself into family time instead of hibernating into the bedroom behind a computer screen. Pride prevented him from admitting how much he missed the friendship he once shared with Kayla.

"Hey, Ashley," he greeted, standing next to the display she was working on. "Is the boss around?" Her conservative attire confirmed Sam's earlier conversation with Bobby Chen Li. Today was the first time ever seeing Ashley in a skirt that reached her knees, and her makeup was more modest.

"Hey, Pastor Jerrod," she answered, after leaning over her shoulder. "Those are beautiful," she added, after turning completely around. Sam was carrying a dozen red roses.

Sam took note of the contentment veiling her countenance. Ashley radiated what Sam called the joy of the Lord. The exact kind of joy that would make one stop living in sin. "Thanks. I hope the boss lady likes them."

"The boss lady is pleased," Kayla answered, behind Sam.

It worked, Sam thought. The sheer happiness resting on Kayla's face guaranteed another peaceful night in the Jerrod household. "Hey, beautiful." Her beauty shone through her selfishness.

She tiptoed and kissed his lips. "Thank you. Come on back to my office and I'll show you some gratitude." She winked, then sniffed the flowers.

Sam had an appointment with Danté's teacher in forty-five minutes, but thought it better not to mention it to Kayla. To keep the peace, he'd give her thirty minutes of his undivided attention, then speed across town.

Sam offered her his free arm. "Whatever, you say, boss lady."

Chapter 21

"Good morning," Kayla sang, when her men entered the kitchen for breakfast. Saturdays had become her favorite day of the week now that she had them off. In preparing Ashley to run the store while she's on maternity leave, Kayla handed the weekend reigns over. Her first Lamaze class that evening made today extra special. "How was the marina?"

"Breezy, but sunny," Sam answered. After a quick peck and embrace, his hands lingered, stroking her belly.

Kayla still hadn't gotten used to Danté's hand trailing Sam's. She couldn't tell if Danté genuinely enjoyed feeling the baby move, or if he were simply indulging Sam. He only started after Sam coaxed him, and he only did it in Sam's presence. The kid was good. "Hey, little brother," he'd say. Dialogue with Kayla had expanded to about twelve words when Sam wasn't home.

Kayla patted their hands then moved away. "Breakfast will be ready in five minutes." She had packed the day with shopping for the baby shower with her mother before Lamaze class.

Sam and Danté left and returned to the table in matching outfits—blue jeans, gold hoodies and sunglasses. "Y'all are too cool for me," Kayla said, while shaking her head. "Now eat up."

"Aren't you eating?" Sam asked, when she started out of the kitchen.

"Mama and I are going to stop for brunch to fuel up before shopping," she announced over her shoulder, but kept walking.

"Just try not to buy everything in the store. Leave something for the other customers."

"Don't worry about us." Her neck rolled. "Just make sure you're on time for our big date." She grabbed her purse and headed out the door into the garage. Getting behind the wheel had become a chore. First, she had to move the seat back, then ease in sideways, before tugging the seatbelt into place. On the way to her mother's house, she phoned and reminded Carlos he promised to supervise Danté tonight while she and Sam attended Lamaze.

Besides childbirth class, tonight would be the first time she and Sam would enjoy an evening out in weeks. Sam didn't know it, but after Lamaze, he was treating her to dinner and a movie in the park. They needed to reconnect before the baby came. They'd been dwelling peacefully, more like tolerating one another. Sam made sporadic mediocre efforts to work on their relationship, but it was evident his heart wasn't in it. She couldn't recall the last time the words "I love you" were uttered by either of them. Tonight, that would change.

∞

"Mija, would you please stop pacing before you work yourself into a frenzy!" Carlos pleaded for the second time.

It was too late. Kayla was already in a frenzy of worry. She couldn't stop pacing in the living room if she wanted to. Sam was an hour late and his phone went straight to voicemail the five times she called. They were minutes from missing Lamaze class. They could reschedule if another class opened before her due date, but not if Sam were hurt.

"Try calling his phone again," she ordered, as she whisked past.

"I just did." Carlos clipped his phone, then pulled out his keys. "Where did they go, to the church? I'll check and see if they are there?"

Kayla silently whizzed by.

"Mija!" Carlos gripped her shoulders on the trip back and held her stationary. "Where were they supposed to go today?"

Her brother may as well have been speaking a foreign language. Kayla didn't have an answer. She'd left out that morning not caring what their plans were as long as they were back in time for her agenda.

"I don't know."

"What?"

"Don't look at me like that," she snapped, attempting to slap his hands away. "I was too busy with my plans to ask."

His brow furrowed. "Explain to me how you being the spoiled and nosey brat that you are, don't know how your husband and son spend their time?"

"Don't judge me!" This time she pushed his chest. "My husband could be laying in a ditch somewhere bleeding to death. I have to find him." She grabbed her keys and started for the door.

He grabbed her arm. "Mija, wait! We'll find them, but let's be smart. Doesn't his cell phone have a tracking device? I know you have the password to his account."

Kayla's eyes rolled. "Shut up." She began signing into Sam's account, praying the phone was nearby. "I can't believe it." Her breath caught. "He's in San Francisco."

"What's going on in the city?"

The pacing resumed as her fear turned into anger. "How the heck should I know? I can't think of one reason why he would go to the city knowing we have Lamaze today." The clock on her phone confirmed they would miss their class.

"At least now you know where they are."

"He and his son can stay there for all I care, especially since he won't answer my calls."

"Maybe his phone is dead, or maybe he's somewhere where he had to turn the phone off."

"He should be here!"

"And you're yelling at me because…" He let the question hang.

"Because you're here and he's not!" Kayla rarely yelled at her older brother, but tonight was supposed to be her time, and Sam ruined it.

Carlos started for the door. "Since you won't be needing me to watch my nephew, I'm going to surprise Jasmine with dinner and a movie."

"So, you're just going to leave me?"

He gripped the door handle before looking over his shoulder and responding. "Yes, I am. And I suggest you calm down before your husband gets back. Obviously, there's been a miscommunication. Try not to tear his head off without hearing him out." Then he was gone.

The pacing didn't stop until dusk when Kayla finally sat down on the couch in defeat. Part of her was hoping Sam would make it back in time to salvage some of the evening. She could endure labor without Lamaze, but needed Sam's attention and affirmation that he still found her attractive. Maybe the increase in hormones fueled her insecurities, but the inflated wide face and swollen ankles combined with the twenty pounds she'd gained, yielded an unfavorable self-image. She longed to feel cherished and desired again, and not just tolerated. The only way that could happen was if she and Sam spent intimate time together. Maybe she'd waited too long to revive their relationship. Maybe they would forever remain out of sync. Tears she did not want to shed pooled and trickled down her cheeks until she heard the garage door open.

Before the door dividing the house and garage opened, Kayla rubbed her face dry and reigned in her emotions. Like Carlos said, it could all be a simple miscommunication. A few minutes later, Sam entered the living room with Danté in tow. Both were carrying a bag filled with what appeared to be games.

"Hey, sweetheart. How did the shopping and party planning go? Did you clean the store out?" When he leaned in to kiss her cheek, his cell phone came into view, confirming his phone wasn't lost or stolen.

"Where did you go today?" she asked, not wanting him to know she'd tracked his phone.

"I promised Danté I'd take him to the junior gaming tournament when it came to San Francisco. I meant to be back earlier, but we were having such a great time."

"Oh, really?" Kayla's cheeks warmed, indicating she'd lose the battle to control her temper real soon.

"You should have seen our boy playing against some of the best gamers in his age group." Sam beamed with pride. "I didn't know he was that good. Next year, I'm sure he'll place."

Her left carotid artery pulsated as she measured her words. "So, you spent the day and half the evening playing video games?"

"We had a great time. Maybe you can come with us next year."

The pride on Sam's face combined with Danté's smirk was her undoing. It took her a moment to maneuver from the couch and stand. She made no attempt to control the anger and the hurt motivating her.

"You missed the Lamaze class it took weeks to get, so you could play videos games with him?" She pointed at Danté. "How stupid could I have been, thinking you cared anything about me or this baby."

"What?"

She invaded his personal space as much as her extended belly would allow and pointed at his chest. Her neck rolled mechanically. "I spent the past few hours worried about you because you didn't answer your phone. And you were playing video games? I could have gone into labor. What's worse is you weren't man enough to tell me you didn't want to attend Lamaze. I could have asked Carlos to be my labor partner. My brother has never let me down like you have. All you care about is kissing Danté's royal—"

"Kayla! Not in front of Danté."

The force of Sam's voice made her pause, but only for a second. "I don't care about his feelings. The boy barely speaks to me. He doesn't care about me, and apparently neither do you. You've negated me to third place, after a video game."

Sam's temporal vein pulsated and his nostrils flared, but Kayla refused to back down.

"Danté, go to your room," Sam ordered, without turning away from Kayla.

Danté ran down the hallway without uttering a word.

Still glaring at her, Sam unclipped his phone, then started for their bedroom. "My phone is dead. I forgot to charge my phone last night, and ran out this morning without the car charger."

She followed. He wasn't getting off that easy. "When did you find that out? Was it before, or after you missed the Lamaze class? I bet you didn't even remember. I'm not a priority to you," she charged from behind, while he inserted the charger and powered up the phone. I'm tired of begging you for attention. Maybe if I put a game controller in my hand, I'd get a spot on your calendar."

Sam whirled around. "Will you shut up! Get off your high horse and try listening for once. Everything is not about you."

The sudden action and roar threw Kayla off-balance. She stepped backward until the back of her legs touched the bed.

"I've had it with your selfish behavior and complaining, always wanting things your way." His pointed finger missed her forehead by a hair. "I do everything possible to keep peace in this house, and all you do is find fault with me. It's fine if you hate me, it won't kill me. But you just attacked a child because of your mistake."

"The only mistake I made was marrying you."

"I didn't actually win the lottery with you either," he shot back. "You're not perfect, Kayla, far from it." He thrust the phone in her face. "Lamaze is next week. You just told the child you vowed to love and raise as your own that you don't care about him, all because you got your dates mixed up. How is he supposed to feel? He already lost one mother."

She looked down at the screen displaying Sam's calendar. His calendar showed the right time, but the wrong day. "You're the one with the wrong date. You probably weren't listening when I told you. I should have told Danté then maybe you would have gotten it right."

"Stop! Grow up and take responsibility," Sam roared, throwing the phone across the room in the process. "You're the one who added it to my calendar because you didn't trust me to do it, remember?"

Kayla turned away. She did remember adding Lamaze to Sam's phone, but doubted she selected the wrong date.

"You can't admit when you're wrong; grow up and stop competing with Danté and lying about how much he hates you. You've been doing that since he got here, and I'm tired of it. It's pathetic to see a grown woman jealous of a kid."

She whirled around. "I am not lying! I am not jealous. He barely speaks to me when you're not here."

"And you barely speak to either of us unless it benefits you. You've divided this family into us against you, and I'm sick and tired of it." He stormed away, but abruptly turned back. "And another thing, if you're that satisfied with how well your brother treats you, then marry him! Don't ever compare me to him or any other man again. If you're that unhappy, leave."

Her heart sank. "That's what you want isn't it? You want me to leave."

"What I want is for you to stop whining and complaining and to at least pretend you like having Danté around before the baby comes. He's experienced too much trauma already in his short life. I don't want him feeling like he's not loved."

"What about me? When will I feel loved around here? I know he came before me, but I am the one you made vows to."

"You can start by admitting you screwed up today and apologize to Danté."

Her head shook violently. "Today was not my fault. I know I didn't mark the wrong day. I had dinner planned and everything."

"Of course, nothing is ever your fault," he said, patronizing her. "I knew you were a drama queen before I married you, but this is ridiculous." His hands raised in surrender. "I give up."

"No, I quit," Kayla rebutted without considering the severity of her next words. "I refuse to compete anymore with a kid for my husband's attention. If you're not man enough to admit a video game is more important to you than spending time with me, you're not worth the effort. I'm done."

Kayla couldn't read his thoughts in the silence that followed. His eyes were so cold as if flirting with the thin line that separates love and hate. They were at a point of no return and she didn't care.

"Do whatever you want," he finally said. "I'm going to try and repair the emotional damage you've done to my son."

The second after he slammed the bedroom door, Kayla wobbled to the closet and rolled out a suitcase. She had to get out of that house before she lost what little self-control she had left. The happy life she'd once known was over. She'd lost the battle and was conceding the war. Her heart felt like it would burst with every item she threw into the suitcase, but the baby's movements kept her composed, being the one bright spot in her life.

She could only hope the items she blindly piled into the wheeled suitcase would be sufficient enough to sustain her until she sorted out a plan for her life without Sam.

The trek down the hallway with the suitcase trailing behind halted when she remembered something. She rushed back to the master bath and lotioned her fourth finger on her left hand. After removing her wedding ring, she left it on Sam's vanity, then hurried out the door, effectively closing the door of her heart.

Chapter 22

"You seem distracted. Are you alright?" Tyrell whispered the question after Sam failed to respond to an inquiry from the church secretary during the morning administrative meeting.

Sam was not alright, but as a leader in the church, he could not air his marital problems. At least that's what his problems were twenty-four hours ago when he had a marriage. The fallout with Kayla had been epic, and at the time he couldn't stand to be in her presence. In a few short months she'd transformed into a selfish person he wasn't sure he liked. She'd crossed the line with Danté last night, but he never expected her to pack up and leave simply because things didn't go her way. Astonished didn't begin to describe his reaction to seeing her wedding ring on his vanity and an empty section in her half of the closet when he returned to their bedroom this morning. After consoling Danté, he'd spent the night in the den. How dare she wreak havoc and then jump ship.

Focusing on her actions helped him discount the pain caused by her sudden departure. When he declared his wedding vows, he meant them until death. In good and bad times. Apparently, Kayla did not.

He shook his head as to clear it. "I'm fine. What did I miss?"

"Minister Higgins can fill you in later," Pastor Simmons answered for Tyrell. "It's time to pray and prepare for service. Minister Chavez can take over your duties today."

Sam swallowed hard at the subtle, but stern rebuke from Pastor Simmons. He bowed his head to keep from making eye contact. The last thing he needed was for his pastor to discern his administrative pastor couldn't successfully administrate his own home.

Pastor Simmons sermon brought conviction to Sam. He and Kayla needed to talk, but honestly, he didn't know how to make her understand his point of view. And although he loved her, he could not and would not tolerate her mistreating Danté. Alone in their bedroom after service, Sam released his pride enough to call his wife, only to be greeted by voicemail. After leaving several messages, she finally returned his call. Her ringtone made him pause and pray before answering in case he was presented with more drama.

"Babe, I—"

She cut him off. "We're done. The only thing connecting us is the baby. Since you're a much better father than husband, I'll keep you informed about the baby and let you know when I go into labor, but that's it. Stop calling me, it's too stressful. After the baby is born, we can discuss dissolving the marriage. Until then, don't call me, I'll call you."

His voice lodged in his throat as his mind dissected the real message.

"Do you understand what I'm saying?" she continued. "It's going to take all of my time and energy reorganizing my life and starting over on my own. I'll be sure to pick up the rest of my clothes and the baby's stuff at times you're not there. As for church, I'll let you figure that out. Just know I won't be there."

The pounding in his chest was so intense, Sam had to remind himself to breathe. "So, you've decided our marriage is over. Just like that?"

"I'm not going to argue about our marriage anymore. I tried hard to be the wife you needed and a mother for Danté, but it just wasn't good enough. We're on two different paths. We made a mistake, but what's done is done. I just want to move on and do what's best for my baby. Goodbye."

Sam's eyes frantically roamed the bedroom, not really seeing anything. He didn't have to see her face to know Kayla was serious. Right or wrong, she'd made up her mind. Her rejection demolished his pride and crushed his heart. Despite her faults, he loved her wholeheartedly and wanted to spend the rest of his life with her. The line went dead before he could gather his thoughts and voice what was in his heart.

The phone slipped from his hand as he fell back onto the bed with his palms rubbing his forehead. What had just happened? The past seven months had been a rollercoaster ride, and honestly, there were days he wanted to get off, but the thought was always fleeting. Did she really say she was moving out? He bolted upright, stood and began pacing. We're divorcing? What does she mean, we're on different paths? What's happening to my life? The questions hung in the air. "This can't be real," he voiced, looking at Kayla's side of the bed. "She's not coming back?" The declaration sent tremors through him.

"Dad, what's for dinner? Can we order pizza?"

Sam spun around to find Danté's expectant eyes, and prayed his own eyes didn't reveal his turmoil. He hadn't planned for dinner, thinking after he and Kayla made up, she would decide what they were eating. Kayla was gone and wasn't coming back.

"Sure, I'll call in an order."

"Cool." Danté grinned and left the room without asking about Kayla's whereabouts.

After calling in the order, Sam collapsed on the bed and wept.

Chapter 23

"Ma," Kayla called from the foyer of her mother's house. The dead silence yielded Kayla the opportunity to move into the spare bedroom without her mother looking over her shoulder interrogating her. Upon leaving home six years ago, Kayla vowed never to live under her mother's roof again. She loved her mother, but valued her independence more. Now, not only was she moving back in, but in ten weeks, adding a baby. Not her ideal situation, but after hibernating in a hotel for three days this was the more economical solution. Spending $125 per night was not the way to save for an apartment. Plus, she would need her mother's help with the baby. Rozelle had already agreed to care for the baby once she returned to work. This living arrangement would make it more convenient, Kayla reasoned, pushing the wheeled suitcase down the hall.

Reorganizing her life, she could handle, but explaining to Rozelle about the breakup with Sam would be laborious. Rozelle loved Sam like a son and would not agree with the new path Kayla had chosen. Alone in the hotel the first night, Kayla doubted her decision. There was some truth to the drama queen label Sam placed on her, and sometimes she spoke without thinking. The comment about not caring about Danté wasn't from the heart, but out of frustration. Even so, Sam didn't apologize and ask her to come back. She wouldn't have done so, but would have had the satisfaction of knowing he was in pain. They had grown so far apart in such a short period of time, she didn't know him anymore. Accusing her of lying proved he didn't know her either. When he proposed, he promised never to love anyone more than her. He broke that promise the day Danté moved in.

"Calm down, sweetie." Kayla took a break from stocking the drawers and soothed the baby by rubbing her belly. The baby movements seem to have increased since leaving her home. She wondered if her unborn child could sense her emotional turmoil. Did the fetus miss Sam's daily strokes and tenor lullabies? Stubbornness prevented Kayla from admitting she missed her husband's touch.

"Kayla, are you here?"

She jumped at her mother's voice, then quickly recovered. At the slightest sign of weakness, Rozelle would tear down Kayla's resolve, brick by brick.

"I'm in the guest room."

"The guest room?" The voice drew closer.

"You can do this." Kayla gave herself a pep talk while doing a quick breathing exercise.

"I was surprised to see your car outside. I thought we we're going to wait until the weekend to work on the favors." Rozelle stood in the doorway.

Kayla zipped up the suitcase. "I decided to come by early. Actually, I'm moving in." No use in beating around the bush, she thought with her back to her mother.

"Excuse me?"

"Not forever," Kayla clarified. "Just until after I recover from having the baby and find an apartment. I'm thinking no more than three months."

"And I'm thinking I didn't give you a spare key to run away from your husband and child."

Here we go. She turned around and looked in her mother's direction, but did not make eye contact. "I know you don't understand, but I can't take living in that house anymore with those two. The bottom line is Sam and I made a mistake, we should have never gotten married."

Rozelle stepped completely into the room. "Come again."

Kayla made it as plain as possible. "Ma, I know you love Sam; I love him," she admitted, "but he's a lousy husband and I can't be with him anymore. I need to focus on me and my baby. He and Danté will be fine."

Rozelle's facial expression changed several times, Kayla could only guess her thoughts.

"You're serious." Rozelle sat on the bed and patted the space next to her. "Baby, sit down and tell me what's really going on."

Here goes nothing. Kayla obeyed and exposed how miserable she'd been since Danté moved in and how she and Sam had grown apart and lived more like roommates than husband and wife. To her surprise, her mother didn't interrupt, but simply listened and nodded.

"I see. Have you prayed about this?" she asked, after a prolonged silence.

Kayla hadn't prayed about leaving Sam. In fact, she hadn't prayed about her marriage in a long time. She and Sam used to pray together every morning, but that ceased when the feuding started. It's hard to pray with someone and not be on speaking terms.

"In order for prayer to work, both parties must be willing," she answered, without saying she was the one not willing.

Rozelle nodded. "I see you've thought about this."

"Yes. I've made up my mind."

"One of the things I don't understand is why you left your house. Why isn't Sam the one looking for a new residence?"

Kayla knew what she meant, and although she was done with Sam, she didn't want her mother to have harsh feelings. "I made the decision to leave. When Sam and I purchased the house, it was with our future family in mind. Since we're no longer a unit, I don't want the house."

Rozelle's eyebrows knitted and Kayla waited for her mother to declare her certifiably crazy.

"Okay. Wow. Well, Travis and I don't mind you staying here, but I do hope you and Sam will reconcile."

That's it? "Don't waste your time watering a dead rose."

Rozelle nodded some more before standing up. "I'm going to call and let Travis know our empty nest is no longer empty." She started toward the threshold. "After dinner, we can start on the favors."

Kayla looked up at the ceiling and exhaled a huge sigh of relief, after her mother was gone. Now that she'd gotten her mother to see things her way, she could focus on the new chapter in her life.

Chapter 24

Normally, Sam would have answered the phone on the first ring. The ringtone he'd assigned to his mother always brought a smile to his face, but today wasn't normal. How could he tell his mother his marriage was ending? He was still having a hard time digesting a reality he never envisioned. It was still all a blur to him. He'd thought back numerous times to when Kayla first met Danté, before they were dating. She instantly fell in love with him and spoiled him. She knew he and Danté were a package deal. She even promised Sherri she'd raise him. When house hunting, Kayla insisted on a home with a backyard in a family-friendly neighborhood. So why all the disdain now? What gave her the right to unilaterally decide the marriage was over?

The ringtone stopped only to start again. Avoiding Stella Jerrod was not an option. She would call until he answered, or be on a flight from Chicago to see what was going on. He couldn't allow that to happen.

He cleared his throat and tried to sound normal. "Hey, Mama. How are you?"

"What on earth is going on with you and Kayla? Why has she moved out?"

Sam swallowed hard. How did she know? She was a praying woman; had the Lord revealed it to her. Or, had Kayla told her?

She answered the question for him. "Rozelle called me this morning, saying Kayla had lost what little sense she had, and that we need to pray for y'all. I want to hear it from you. Why is your pregnant wife living with her mother? What is going on in that house?"

Sam exhaled and rubbed his forehead. How could he answer without making Kayla look bad?

"Mama, I don't know." That was the truth. This Kayla was not the woman he married.

"Samuel Jerrod, it's your responsibility to know what's going on in your house and with your wife. How can you lead God's people when you can't take care of the wife He gave you? A woman doesn't give up on her family without a valid cause. She doesn't wake up one morning out of the blue and decide to leave. What have you done, or didn't do that you should have done?"

Sam shook his head in disbelief. His mother blamed him. He'd done everything he thought necessary to keep Kayla happy.

She continued. "Son, I know you're hurting because you love Kayla, but you need to do whatever it takes to get your wife back home. Don't let pride destroy your family."

"What pride?"

"Son, now is not the time to play games. I know you. You're driven to be a good father because you didn't have one. You vowed to love and cherish Kayla until death in good and bad times. After her ordeal, you wanted to be the one to protect her and show her what love is. But, for some reason now, your pride is holding you back. Get on your knees and pray for deliverance before you lose everything."

For the first time ever, Sam wanted to hang up on his mother. This was not his fault. He fulfilled his vows. At least that's what he'd been feeding his psyche since Kayla left.

"Mama, I have to go."

"I know you don't want to hear this, but do whatever it takes to keep your family together."

"I hear you." He wanted her off the phone.

"Son, do more than hear, listen." With that Stella ended the call.

Sam buried his head in his hands on his desk to keep from yelling. His mother demanded he do exactly what he'd been trying to do all along—keep his family together. "God, I need you," he groaned.

"Are you okay?"

My God, can today get any worse? he thought when he heard Pastor Simmons' voice. He'd been avoiding him since the last administrative meeting, but he couldn't keep his marital dilemma a secret forever.

After a deep breath, Sam raised his head with a smile. "Hello, Pastor? How are you this morning?"

Pastor Simmons stepped through the office threshold. "I'm good. Is everything good with Kayla and the baby? I assumed that's why you were distracted on Sunday when Kayla missed the meeting and worship service. I don't recall seeing her at Bible Study last night either."

Sam hesitated, before answering. Since he couldn't lie, he told a half-truth. "Sorry about Sunday. My thoughts were definitely on Kayla. She and the baby are fine now." Just not with me, he wanted to add, but didn't.

"So why do you look like you haven't slept in days?"

Sam threw his hands up along with the façade. "Because I haven't."

"Want to talk about it?"

For a split-second, Sam considered leveling with his mentor, then retreated. He had experienced enough rejection for one week. He looked at the time on his phone. "Maybe later, I have a home visit for communion, in thirty minutes."

"When you're ready, I'm just a phone call away." Pastor Simmons retreated toward the door. "Are you still able to attend the meeting in Sacramento on Thursday, or should I make other arrangements?"

"No, sir, I'll be there. I plan to drive up right after I drop Danté off at school."

"If you can have a report ready for the next administrative meeting that would be great."

Sam waited until he was certain Pastor Simmons was clear of his office, before rounding his desk and closing his office door. He needed to repent for his half-truth before offering communion.

Chapter 25

Doubt paralyzed Kayla the second she entered her code into the keypad of the keyless lock. Formulating a plan was one thing, but executing a plan that would thrust her into a life she never envisioned proved harder than expected. Once she completely moved out of the house, there would be no turning back. As a final test, she waited three days for Sam to call and beg her to come back, but he hadn't. Sure, she told him not to call, but he never listened to her. She would not have answered his calls, but he could have tried. His lack of pursuit cemented her position that he had chosen Danté over her.

To stall, Kayla walked back to the mailbox and looked inside. Nothing. She looked around the yard at nothing in particular, remembering the day they moved in. She and Sam were supposed to grow old in this house. Then came memories of her and Sam christening every room. "Don't go there." She forced her mind to the task at hand

and started toward the door with renewed determination. She had roughly three hours to pack up the rest of her and the baby's belongings while the house was empty.

"What are you doing here?" she asked, when she passed by the den. She'd purposefully chosen the day and time knowing Sam had a meeting in Sacramento. Danté was supposed to be at school, but here he was in the den playing video games.

Startled by her sudden appearance, he jumped up, dropping the game controller in the process.

"What are you doing here?" she asked again, while he looked nervously around the room then picked up the controller.

"I live here. Why are you here?" He plopped back down on the couch.

"This is my—" Kayla stopped short of claiming the house she no longer desired to live in. "Why aren't you at school?"

"I don't have school today."

"Oh really?" She folded her arms. "Then why are you wearing your school uniform?"

Danté threw the controller onto the couch. "That's none of your business!" he yelled. "You don't care about me, or my dad. You left us; so don't worry about what we do."

Her mouth hung as he stood there daring her to contradict him.

"I heard you tell my dad you don't want to live with us anymore. So why are you here? I wish you would leave us alone."

Kayla couldn't deny the truth, even if spoken to cover up the fact that he was cutting school while Sam was in Sacramento for the day. Danté's behavior was Sam's problem, so she resumed her mission.

"Wish granted." She whisked past him and toward the bedroom. To her relief, he didn't follow her. Once inside the bedroom, remorse over the words she'd spoken in anger toward Danté surfaced. She did care, that's what made leaving so hard, but his rejection fueled her determination.

Three suitcases and several bags were stuffed when the high-pitched piercing sound filled the house. Kayla froze, but only for a brief second, then took off running toward the opposite side of the house. Halfway there she smelled and saw smoke coming from the kitchen. What she didn't see in her peripheral vision was Danté on the couch in the den.

Kayla came to a screeching halt at the archway leading into the kitchen. "Oh, my, God!" she screamed. Flames consumed the stove and part of the counter, but what terrified her was the sight of Danté's little body standing on a chair trying to conquer the flames with a gallon bottle of water.

"Danté, get out of here!"

When he kept dodging flames and throwing water, it occurred to Kayla he could not hear her over the fire alarm. She sprinted to the chair and grabbed him from behind, causing more water to spill out on the floor. She turned with the intent to exit through the patio sliding door, but two steps in, she slipped on a puddle and fell.

Danté went one way. She went the other, banging her head on the granite floor.

"Ouch!" She gripped her stomach, more concerned about the baby growing inside her than her head. Dazed, she attempted to get on her knees, but the pain in her head was too excruciating. She fell onto her back. Amidst the smoke and flames she saw Danté crawling toward her.

"Get out of here. Get out of the house now," she ordered, through labored breath, while trying to scoot toward the patio. The smoke was starting to irritate her lungs, or maybe she just noticed. Her ankle throbbed.

"No! I'm not leaving you!" he screamed back, between coughs. "Come on!"

She felt him tugging her arm, like he was trying to drag her. His ten-year-old body was no match for her body weight.

Dizziness made it impossible to hold her head up. "Get out of here, I'll be fine. Help is coming. Go outside and wait." She wasn't sure if it was fire trucks she heard, or if the noise was all in her head. All she knew was she had to get him out of that house before they both burned.

"I'm not leaving you!"

As the pain in her head increased, the groggier she became, the dizzier she felt. The more smoke, the more coughing and more tugging. Her last vision, before losing consciousness, was of tears streaming down Danté's cheeks and his lips mouthing words she could not decipher.

Chapter 26

"Where's my wife!" Sam yelled at the security guard seated behind the desk in the emergency room lobby. "Where is she?" He banged on the raised desk, when she didn't respond. He didn't care that he was dressed in clergy attire, or that he'd illegally parked in a handicapped space after driving nearly ninety miles an hour down Interstate 80 from Sacramento. He had to get to Kayla. Nothing else mattered once he received Rozelle's frantic call telling him the house had caught fire with Kayla and Danté inside.

A firm grip on his shoulder prevented him from causing a greater scene. "She's still being evaluated."

Sam jerked around into Pastor Simmons' face. He didn't find solace in his spiritual leader's presence. Neither did his in-law and best friend bring comfort. He needed to see his wife before he had a mental breakdown.

"Have they said anything? Is she going to be alright?" His head dropped into his cupped hands. "Oh, God, she has to be alright…" His voice trembled, so he stopped speaking.

"Son, she will be, and so will the baby," Pastor Simmons assured him. "Come on, let's sit down, the doctor should be out soon."

Any other time Sam would have appreciated his pastor's unwavering faith, but the state of his marriage rendered him unsure of most things. The one thing he was sure of was he needed his wife to be okay.

He obeyed, and after walking to the opposite side of the crowded room, slumped in a chair between Pastor Simmons and Tyrell. Rozelle sat directly across from him alongside her husband with her head bowed, no doubt praying. The thinly padded chair was too small for his tall frame to be comfortable. After shifting and adjusting positions, Sam gave up and settled on pacing, then abruptly stopped. At that moment, he would give his life for one of Kayla's drama-filled pacing episodes.

"What's taking so long?" Feeling suffocated, he yanked off the clergy collar and stuffed it in his pocket. He paced some more before realizing someone was missing. "Where's Danté, is he okay?" he asked no one in particular.

Glances passed between his family and friends, like they were privy to information he wasn't.

"Carlos took him to the chapel to pray," Rozelle finally answered for the group.

Sam didn't have time to inquire more. Kayla's obstetrician, Dr. Kaur, emerged through the double automatic doors with another medical team member following behind. He rushed to her.

"Doctor, my wife?" Realizing he had stepped into her personal space, he leaned back. "How is she? Please tell me she's okay."

Before Dr. Kaur could answer, everyone had huddled around Sam. When she hesitated, he gestured for her to continue.

"She's good. Not quite where I would like her to be, but good. She suffered a grade four concussion from the fall, meaning she lost consciousness for longer than a minute."

He gasped. "Oh my God."

Dr. Kaur pointed to and introduced her colleague to the group. "This is Dr. Patton, the neurologist."

Dr. Patton briefly greeted the group, before reporting Kayla scored 14 out of 15 on the Glasgow scale, which meant her level of consciousness was good.

Sam exhaled but only partially.

Dr. Kaur continued. "She inhaled a lot of smoke and is on oxygen to help clear and open her lungs. She's mildly sedated to keep her from getting too excited. We need her to rest. Every time she wakes up, she becomes frantic and calls for someone named Danté."

"And the baby?" Sam whispered the question.

"There weren't any direct injuries from the fall. Her cervix is in tack, no amniotic fluid is leaking. The baby's heart rate is normal and the fetal stress test results are good. We will continue monitoring for any changes."

"Thank God." Sam finally fully exhaled. His love would recover and their unborn child would survive. All he had to do now was make things right between them. He'd beg if he had to. "When can I see her?"

"I'm admitting her overnight as a precaution. As soon as she's settled into a bed, I'll have the nurse come and get you," Dr. Kaur explained. "She'll be on the fourth floor; you can wait there."

His nod communicated the words his mouth could not formulate.

Dr. Kaur nodded her understanding then departed with her colleague following behind.

With Pastor Simmons' pat on the back, Sam's inward thoughts joined in with the praises to God his family and friends offered up, but his praise was cut short. He needed to get to Kayla. "I'm going upstairs to wait," he announced, then started for the elevator. When he pressed the call button his confusion returned. "Why did Kayla pick Danté up from school today?" he turned and asked the group. "How did the fire start?"

His pastor, best friend and in-laws shared glances between themselves, but no one made eye contact with him.

"Well, does anyone know?" he pressed, as the elevator chimed.

"Son," Rozelle offered. "When Carlos gets back with Danté you'll understand."

"Understand what?"

"Dad!"

Familiar little hands hugged Sam's waist from behind. He turned and knelt. The fear on Danté's face directed toward him was foreign. He looked upward to Carlos, and then to the group for an answer, but none came.

Danté latched on to Sam's neck and buried his head in Sam's chest. "It's my fault. I'm sorry."

The words were almost undecipherable through his sobs. Danté had been through enough trauma, Sam couldn't let him bear responsibility for Kayla's accident too.

Sam squeezed him. "Son, this is not your fault—"

"Yes, it is," he cut him off. "I did it. Don't hate me, please." His cries filled the waiting room and lobby, prompting the security officer to issue a warning for them to lower their voices.

Once again, Sam looked to the adults for clarification. "What is he talking about?"

"Son, have a seat. Danté has something he needs to tell you. Something that you need to pay attention to and really hear."

Sam obeyed Pastor Simmons' gentle command and walked back to a chair with Danté still clinging to him. He needed to get to Kayla, but Danté's brokenness constrained him and Pastor Simmons' choice of words disturbed him. What did everyone know that he didn't?

Rozelle pulled tissues from her purse and helped Danté to somewhat clean his face after Sam sat down and beckoned him to do the same. Danté chose to stand with his head down, shaking.

Sam lifted his head. "What is it, son? Tell me what happened today."

"I was cooking hot dogs and the towel caught on fire when I was playing PlayStation. I didn't mean to." His voice quavered. "I was in a hurry to get back to the game; I accidently threw the towel on the stove."

"What? Why were you cooking?" Sam shook his head as to clear it. "Wait, why were you at home? I dropped you off at school this morning."

Danté's head fell again. "I waited in the bathroom for a while then walked home. You said you wouldn't be back in town until late. I wanted to practice my games."

"You don't have an access code to the lock, how did you get in?"

"I know your code. I saw the numbers you used. They're the same numbers you use to unlock your phone."

Sam swallowed hard and hoped his face hid the incredulity of it all. The son he perceived as innocent and helpless was bold enough to steal his password and cut school at age ten. He nodded. "Go, on."

"Miss Kayla was packing her clothes when the fire started. I tried to put it out, but it was too big. She fell when she tried to pick me up." More sniffles. "I tried to pull her out, but she was too heavy. I don't want her and the baby to die. I don't want to lose another mother."

"The firemen said when they arrived, Danté was trying to drag her out of the patio door," Carlos finally spoke.

Relief washed over Sam. Surely Danté's heroic actions would settle Kayla's doubts once and for all. But the reprieve was only temporary.

"It's my fault she left us. It's my fault she doesn't want to live with us anymore. I lied when I told her I didn't want her around. I was mean to her all the time when you weren't home. And I," he paused and sniffled some more. "I changed the calendar on your phone so you would take me to the tournament. I didn't want you to go to that baby class. I wanted you to take me to the tournament. It's my fault she got mad and left. But I don't want her to die. Please don't be mad."

Sam stared at the child as if seeing him for the first time. Danté's admission shattered the pieces of his already-fragile heart to the point, he didn't care that everyone now knew Kayla had left him. He genuinely loved this child as his own, but at that moment he had no words, just thoughts of how much he'd sacrificed and lost because of that love. Mechanically, his hands attempted to stop the heavy tear streaming down Danté's cheeks. "Is there anything else I need to know?' he whispered, to keep his voice from breaking.

Danté's head shook from side to side. "I'm sorry. I won't leave school again. I promise to stop being mean to Miss Kayla."

Sam had to turn away before he broke down. He'd failed in every area that mattered. He didn't have a book or manual to guide him through this turn of events. No scripture came to mind to navigate him down the path of failure. The puddles in his eyes thickened; he had to leave before his internal pain manifested into outward wailing.

"We'll talk about this later," he mouthed more than audibly spoke, then stood and headed for the stairwell.

Chapter 27

The rhythmic sound of his baby's heart beating was the catalyst that kept Sam's sanity intact as he sat by Kayla's bedside. If only his broken heart could beat with the same ease. In just a few days the bottom had fallen out. His world as he knew it no longer existed. Those he loved broke his heart, and he broke the heart of the one he loved most. At some point he needed to see how much damage his home sustained and notify the insurance company, but honestly, he didn't care. The house hadn't been a home since Kayla's departure, five days ago.

"Baby, I'm so sorry," he whispered, and resumed stroking her cheek.

Her rhythmic breathing escalated into moans.

His hand traveled down to her abdomen and rubbed, assuming the baby was causing discomfort and not sure what else to do to soothe her. His efforts proved futile. Every stroke seemed to bring her into a heightened state of consciousness.

Her head tossed from side to side. "Danté. My son," she mumbled.

His hand traveled back to her face. "Baby, he's fine," he whispered. "Relax."

"Where's my son?" Her voice grew stronger and the rambling continued. "Go. Danté."

How could he have ever doubted this woman? Even slightly sedated, her genuine love for Danté shone through. He leaned in and kissed her forehead.

Her eyes flickered open, but the trepidation veiling her eyes hindered Sam from expressing his feelings. Did she need or even want him there?

A few breaths later, Kayla broke eye contact and attempted to rise up on her elbows, then fell back. "Where's Danté? Is he hurt?"

"He's fine. Take it easy," Sam, whispered, concealing his hurt that she hadn't addressed him directly.

Ignoring him, Kayla raised up again, this time looking around the room. "Danté," she called. "Where is he? I want to see him."

"Is everything alright," the nurse asked, entering the room. "Your blood pressure and respirations are going up again."

"Where's my son? Danté!" she called out.

Sam stepped away from the bed, and with ease the nurse got Kayla to calm down with the promise to allow Danté a few minutes to visit. She then addressed Sam, "She's been asking for him since she got here and she's not going to rest until she sees him. Give me a few minutes to review the strip, then bring him in for a short visit."

"Thank you." Sam texted Rozelle to bring Danté to Kayla's room from the waiting room, all the while wondering how his wife would react to Danté's demeanor. Rozelle had texted Sam earlier to say Danté had been crying ever since Sam left them downstairs, nearly an hour ago.

"Your mother is bringing him up now."

Kayla responded by turning her head away toward the opposite wall, effectively communicating nothing had changed between them. Disheartened, Sam went into the hallway to wait for his mother-in-law and son.

∞

Counting her baby's heartbeat proved to be the distraction Kayla needed to keep from yielding to the need in Sam's eyes. Even in her semi-sedated state, she discerned his desire for the comfort and assurance she could no longer give. Sure, he loved her, but he didn't trust her and without that, they had nothing. "Thank you, Jesus," she whispered with gentle strokes against her belly. God had shielded her unborn baby from danger. Shortly, she'd see if that same mercy was extended to the son she tried to love. She didn't know how long ago the fire occurred, but she vividly remembered Danté's raw fear. He hadn't cried so hard since the day Sherri passed away. Kayla's heart broke for him then. Today her heart ached for breaking her promise to Sherri.

"They're here."

Kayla faced the door, but didn't see Danté. Sam's distressed countenance concerned her. "Where is he? Was he hurt?"

"He's fine, but he has something to tell you." As soon as Sam stepped completely into the room, Danté rushed by him and onto Kayla's bed.

"I'm sorry," he cried, with his arms around her neck. "Please don't die."

Kayla cuddled him as best she could with her protruding abdomen. "Hey, I'm so happy to see you. Are you okay?"

He continued as if he hadn't heard her. "I'm sorry for being mean to you. I lied; I do like you. I didn't mean to start the fire. I don't want you and the baby to die."

"The baby and I are fine. So are you, we're all safe now." She stroked his head for assurance, but the sobs and ranting continued.

"But it's my fault. I was mad. I'm sorry for all the mean things I said. I don't want you to leave us. I just wanted to go to the tournament. I'm sorry."

Kayla looked to Sam and her mother for clarity, but none came. Sam lowered his head, almost cowardly, and her mother gestured toward Danté. Kayla lifted his head and looked directly into his fluid-filled eyes. "Baby, slow down and talk to me," she said after cleaning his face with the tissues Rozelle handed her. "I know you didn't start the fire on purpose."

His head shook violently. "It's my fault you fell. I made you leave. I just wanted to go to the tournament. I didn't want you to leave us. I shouldn't have changed Dad's calendar."

The fire and fall, she understood. How Sam's calendar factored in remained a mystery. "What are you talking about?"

He was nearly heaving from crying so hard. "I changed Dad's calendar so he could take me to the tournament. That's why he missed the baby class. And you got mad and left. Then the fire happened and you fell."

Kayla's jaw dropped.

"I lied, Miss Kayla. I do love you. But I love my mom too and she died. I don't want you to take her place. I don't want you to die either. I miss my mom. I don't want to forget her. But I love you—"

"Shush, baby." Kayla pressed his head against her bosom and wrapped her arms around his head and back. Knowing the source of his animosity trampled the brick wall she erected around her heart. It wasn't that he didn't care for her, he just missed his mother. His ten-year-old wisdom couldn't reconcile how to grieve for his mother and care for Kayla at the same time. And she had been too superficial to see past his actions and into his heart. None of the books she'd read on parenting covered the dynamics of a grieving child. She rocked him in her arms until the tremors and heaving subsided. Once again, Rozelle supplied more tissues and Kayla wiped his face.

"I forgive you," she said, tilting his chin with her fingertips. "Please forgive me for the mean things I said. I didn't mean them either. You know I fell in love with you the first night we met and you called me pretty. I don't want to replace your mother. I will never let you forget about your mother. I want you to remember her, celebrate her birthday and any other special things y'all shared. I want you to talk about her. You never have to choose between your mom and me. I promised Sherri I would take care of her baby. I just ask that you give me the chance to keep that promise. We can be as close as you want us to be."

He sniffled and nodded his head. "Okay. I'm sorry," he offered once again before completely cuddling his whole body on the bed next to her. Somehow, he made his narrow body fit around her stomach.

Kayla embraced him. Her heart ached, but unlike in the recent past, the ache she felt was expanding with the love she had for Danté. For the first time, he needed her.

His head popped up. "What's that noise?" he asked as if hearing the baby's heartbeat for the first time.

"That's your baby sister."

The nurse entered after a light knock. "I'm sorry, Mrs. Jerrod, but visiting time is over." She studied the test strip briefly, then waited for Danté to dismount the bed.

Kayla pouted, as the warmth from Danté's body dissipated.

Rozelle grabbed him by the hand. "Come on, let's wait in the waiting room."

Danté's quick peck on the cheek left Kayla blushing. "I love you. See you later." His exiting steps were much lighter than when he entered. "You mean, that's my baby brother making that noise," he corrected, before disappearing.

A huge smile rested on her face while the nurse finished checking her vitals. The smile vanished once she turned her head and saw her husband pressed against the wall. The contrition and agony masking Sam's face required energy she no longer had the desire to exert. She immediately shut her eyes and turned the other way and willed sleep to overtake her.

Chapter 28

While waiting for the elevator his knees buckled and Sam had to palm the wall to keep from falling down. His spirit was no match for the emotional tidal waves and torrential winds ravaging his heart. His emotional life jacket was shredded to pieces by Kayla's rejection. He'd drown any moment if he didn't find his footing.

Observing Kayla and Danté reconcile gave him hope all would be well between him and Kayla. They would soon be a family again. Then cold eyes met his for a brief second before silently being dismissed by the turning of the head. How was he supposed to make amends if she wouldn't even listen to him? Emotionally bankrupt, Sam groaned and banged his head against the wall.

"Have you had enough yet?"

Sam bolted around and found Pastor Simmons just beyond his personal space. "What do you want?" Sam answered, too distraught to guess and too broken to be concerned about displaying disrespect.

"It's time you and I had a talk, man to man."

Now was not the time to hear a lecture about how a man must lead his own house before leading God's people. If Pastor Simmons wanted him to resign from his ministerial duties, then so be it. He had failed at everything else, why should the church be the exception. "I have to survey the damage to my house, and then get Danté settled for the night. Maybe tomorrow." He turned his back to him, indicating the conversation was over.

Pastor Simmons would not be denied; he walked around him. "We will talk tonight. Rozelle took Danté home with her. I will follow you to the house to assess the damage, then you and I will have a long overdue talk."

"I'm drained—"

"Your estranged pregnant wife is in the hospital behind a fire your son caused," Pastor Simmons interrupted. "Now would be a good time to set pride aside."

His pastor mimicked his mother. Sam threw his hands up. "There's no time like the present." He plopped down in a chair after a quick survey of the waiting room. They were alone. "Explain to me how my pride caused the fire. Or tell me how it's all my fault Kayla left me. Go ahead, tell me something I don't already know."

Just as Sam expected, Pastor Simmons ignored his sarcasm and attitude, and sat in the chair directly across from Sam. With them being face-to-face, Sam was forced to maintain eye contact.

"Son," Pastor Simmons began with folded hands. "It's been difficult, but I intentionally have not interfered with your parenting methods. Mainly, because your actions have made it clear my input was not welcomed. I don't take offence that you would rather read parenting books written by strangers who've never raised children than listen to me, because I understand you. And, I respect you as a man." He paused. "I haven't said much about your relationship with Kayla, because you're not comfortable with my role in Kayla's life. To put it plainly, you're jealous of our relationship. I'm simply her spiritual father, just like I'm yours, but I discovered long ago, you want to meet Kayla's spiritual needs exclusively. I don't hold that against you either, because I understand your motivation."

Sam swallowed hard and shifted in his seat, completely exposed. He loved and respected his pastor, and yet he spoke the truth. Sam had secretly resented the fact that it was Pastor Simmons who led Kayla to Christ and taught her Christian principles and not him. Whereas, Kayla blocked Sam, she opened up completely to Pastor Simmons.

"Sam, I love you as a son, but you're a grown man. I have to afford you the respect to run your household as you see fit, which is why I haven't pressed too hard. I made myself available, hoping you would come to me for help on your own. I've been waiting since Sunday for you to tell me Kayla left."

Sam's head shot up.

"Don't look so surprised. Remember, I'm the closest thing she has to a father figure. She called me on Sunday evening and told me everything. It was a cry for help, although, she didn't take my advice. You, on the other hand, pretended like nothing was wrong. Male pride is a powerful thing, and yours won't allow you to peel the layers back and deal with your real issue. Son, it's only by God's mercy you didn't lose your entire family today." He scooted his chair closer. "As your pastor, I must tell you the truth, whether you like it or not."

The pulsating carotid artery in Sam's neck belied his calm outward demeanor. His pastor possessed the sharpest discernment of anyone he knew and was about to excise him like a master surgeon. He choked out the words, "I'm listening."

"Your love for Kayla and Danté is pure. Your desire is to be the best husband and father, and there's nothing wrong with that. The problem is you're trying to emulate something you have never seen imitated. You were reared by a strong single mother, with little to no paternal involvement. You have no idea of the dynamics involved with balancing spousal and parental relationships. That's the main reason I required you and Kayla to attend marriage counseling before marrying you. You are so driven to be the father to Danté you didn't have, you've forgotten the vows you made to Kayla."

"I don't understand," Sam conceded for the first time. In his thinking, he'd kept his vows.

"You and Kayla are one—a unit. She shouldn't have to compete with anyone, not even your children, for your attention. Your wife should always know she's number one in your life, your queen. You were wrong to dismiss her concerns about Danté's behavior. Even if you didn't experience it, your role was to address her concerns then set boundaries for Danté. Your response translated to her that you didn't care about her feelings and that you valued Danté over her. Your actions said, she doesn't matter to you. Once a woman gets to that place, she shuts down. She may physically remain, but her heart closes a little more with each rejection. Kayla may have moved out on Sunday, but I'm sure if you think back, she began drifting away the first time you ignored her concerns."

Sam shifted in the chair, thinking back to the first night of Danté's arrival when he'd overruled the plans Kayla had for dinner in favor of what Danté wanted. His intention wasn't to hurt Kayla, but to make Danté feel welcomed. There was some truth in Pastor Simmons' words.

"You poured your all into Danté and left Kayla vulnerable. Pride prevented you from getting Danté into counseling. You thought you could handle a grieving abused child on your own, but you can't. Blended families are hard enough without death. Prayer is always good, but you also need professional help."

"I was only trying to give Danté a stable home," Sam interrupted. "He deserves a dependable father who won't abuse him."

"True, and Kayla deserves a husband she can depend on. You have to find a balance to do both, especially now. In a few weeks your child will be born. Then what?"

Sam exhaled; this he could handle. "I have been working hard assuring Danté that my love for him won't change once the baby is born. I will always be there for him. He knows that."

"That's great for Danté. Too bad your wife doesn't have that same assurance."

The words dropped from Pastor Simmons' mouth with the force of a sledgehammer. He regretted calling Kayla a selfish liar. What little strength he had left seeped out. His ego shriveled under Pastor Simmons glare. He dropped his head in his hands and discreetly wiped the fluid accumulating in the corners of his eyes.

Pastor Simmons waited for him to look up again then placed a hand on his knee. "Son, God is going to grant you your heart's desire. You will be a great husband and father. And one day you will succeed me once I retire."

Sam's breath caught.

"Don't look so surprised. Why do you think I'm so hard on you? You have a divine calling to lead God's people, and as your spiritual father it's my job to help you fulfill that call. So, as of right now, I'm not asking, but ordering you into one-on-one training sessions with me. I'm going to teach you everything I know about being a godly husband and father. Danté will begin counseling tomorrow with a colleague. When Kayla is ready, you and she will attend marriage counseling with my wife and me."

"But—"

Pastor Simmons' raised open hand silenced him. "This is not open for debate or negotiations. I will no longer sit back and watch you fumble your way through. Your pride won't allow you to ask for help, so I'm pushing it aside for you. You have too much to lose, and I love you too much to watch you fall."

The internal tremors along with the pounding in his chest distracted Sam, allowing the optic rivers to crest and flow downstream before he could stop them. His pastor was too late; Sam had already lost his everything—Kayla.

Pastor Simmons stood and offered his hand to Sam. "Well?"

Instead of reaching for the open hand, Sam dropped his face in his own hands and wept.

Chapter 29

"Remind me never to have you pick out my clothes again," Kayla declared after holding up the five-color ensemble Carlos bought for her trip home from the hospital.

"Really, mija? You have the nerve to insult me after I dropped everything to be at your beck and call." He shook his head. "Ma is right, you are a spoiled brat."

Kayla slid off the bed and waddled toward the bathroom with her toiletries and clothes in hand. "Yeah, but you love me."

"So does Sam, and he's just as responsible as I am for spoiling you."

The unexpected mention of his name immobilized her. "Why do you find it necessary to mention him?"

Carlos walked around her and locked eyes with Kayla. "Because he's your husband, and he should be the one picking you up and taking you to the place he has provided."

She blinked and turned away. She hadn't expected to ever hear her brother take Sam's side on anything.

"Mija, you can't run away from this," he continued. "At some point you're going to have to make things right with Sam.

"I'm sorry you don't understand, but I have to do what's best for me and the baby, and unfortunately Sam's not it." She continued on to the bathroom, too stubborn to admit how much those words saddened her.

Inside the bathroom she busied herself with a quick shower while pondering her next move. She still needed to go by the house and get the rest of her clothes. At least, she hoped she had some clothes left. And what about all of the baby stuff? No one mentioned how much of the house had been destroyed in the fire.

"I can't believe I missed the signs," she voiced to her reflection in the mirror. Danté's confession infiltrated her conscious thoughts all night. Why didn't she realize the cause of his hostility was his grief? As hard as she tried, she couldn't recall any of the child-rearing books she purchased cover his dilemma. She rubbed her stomach, wondering if she would recognize distress symptoms of her little one. At least now Sam knew she wasn't a selfish liar. Maybe now they could find a way to peacefully co-parent after the divorce.

"Ugh!" she shook her head at her reflection. The color ensemble looked hideous on her body. Since she couldn't kneel, Kayla sat on the toilet seat and bowed her head and prayed. God's mercy protected her and Danté from death and the child in her womb. He had proven that He could do anything, and for that she owed Him some praise.

She stepped from the bathroom, rejuvenated. "Okay, bro, let's get out of here. Find the nurse and tell her I'm…"

"Hello, beautiful."

Kayla looked around the room. Her brother was gone. In his stead, Sam stood near the window with his arms behind his back. His countenance more peaceful than yesterday; his posture more erect. His black apparel accentuated muscles she knew every curvature to. She blinked and looked away. "Where's Carlos?"

"He left. I'm taking you home. How are you?"

Kayla made a mental note to punch her brother. He had no right to leave without checking with her first. "You're taking me where?"

"Not to our house. It's uninhabitable until the kitchen and family room are replaced. We're staying in the church apartment building until the cleanup and renovations are completed. The insurance adjuster said it will take at least six weeks." He released his arms and presented a bag with the logo from her favorite sandwich shop. "I brought you a sandwich. I figured you wouldn't eat hospital food."

So, the fire was contained to the kitchen and family room. Her and the baby's clothes had been spared. She accepted the sandwich, without touching him. "Thank you, but I'm going back to Mom's. I do need to pick up my clothes from your house though."

Instead of focusing on the hurt reflected in Sam's eyes, she pressed the nurse call button.

He recovered quickly. "I figured as much. The suitcases you packed are in the car."

Good, they were on the same page. "How's Danté?" Kayla changed the subject to common ground.

"I'm sure your mother is spoiling him to his heart's content." He reached into his back pocket. "Before I forget, here's your phone. I found it in our bedroom."

The nurse entered the room with a wheelchair before Kayla could correct him.

"Ready to check out, Mrs. Jerrod? Just let me review your discharge instructions, then you can be on your way." She turned to Sam. "Mr. Jerrod, you can bring your car around to the main entrance. We'll be down shortly."

Kayla turned her back to Sam and gave the nurse her full attention. Sooner or later, her husband would have to accept the fact that their life together was over.

Thirty minutes later, parked in front of Rozelle's house, he still hadn't gotten the message. On the drive over, he let her eat the sandwich in peace, but had yet to release the power door locks.

"I know you don't want to talk to me, but could you please listen for a few minutes?"

The gentleness in his voice matched the warmth permeating from his palm resting on her shoulder.

"Please. Just hear me out this one time."

"Go ahead," she mumbled, after several long sighs. She rested her hands on her stomach and looked straight ahead. She'd give him her ears, but not her attention.

"Sweetheart, I hurt you and I failed you as a husband. I vowed before God to forsake all others for you, and I broke that vow. It was never my intention to devalue you and make you insecure in your position as my wife. I thought I had everything figured out, but my understanding and perception were totally wrong. I let my desire to give Danté the father's love I never had, blind me to the love and respect due you as my wife. I was out of line for calling you names. You are not a selfish lair, but loving and giving. There is no one else on this earth I would want for the mother of my children. You are, and will always be a drama queen, but that's one of the things I love about you. And, yes, I spoiled you and enjoyed doing so. My mistake was taking my attention away from you and lavishing it all on Danté."

Kayla turned her head to the passenger window. Viewing him through her peripheral vision was too much.

"My ideas on marriage and parenthood were a combination of ideology and fairytale. To be completely honest, I don't know how to be the husband you need and the father our children need, but I am willing to learn. There are many things I am unsure of, many things I ponder and debate in my mind. The one thing I have never wavered on or regretted is, loving you. My world doesn't function without you. I haven't had a full night's sleep since you left. When I got the call about the fire, I thought I had lost you. All of the anger and arguments didn't matter. All I wanted was to hold and protect you. The fire was my fault. If I had not allowed my pride to stop me from coming after you and begging your forgiveness, it wouldn't have happened."

Her head snapped around at that reveal. He had wanted her to come back, but was just as prideful as she was stubborn. When warm fingertips stroked her face, her legs started shaking.

"Sweetheart, I will never allow pride to overrule my love for you again. I'm willing to do whatever I have to, to learn how to be the husband you need, for us to learn how to be a team again. If that means you living with your mother until we can work things out, fine. We can go to counseling, whatever it takes. I just need to know that I have your forgiveness and your love. I promise to give you a better man. Just, please don't give up on me."

She held his pleading stare until squirming joined in with her shaky legs. However heartfelt, his apology was too much to process.

"Baby, please, I—"

She cut him off. "I don't want to deal with this now. Maybe after the baby is born, we can revisit, but not now."

"Can we just agree to try?"

"No," she snapped. "Please unlock the door so I can get out. I got to pee."

His head fell in sync with the power lock release. Before he could get out and walk around to the passenger door, Kayla had maneuvered out and started for the front door. "Tell Danté I'll be back in a few hours to pick him up," he called after her, but she trekked into the house.

Kayla remained in the bathroom long after relieving herself, trying to process Sam's kumbaya performance.

Only it wasn't a performance. Those words flowed from his heart, but didn't have the power to penetrate the wall around hers. When she did make it to the spare bedroom her suitcases were on the bed.

Chapter 30

The final weeks of work before maternity leave proved tougher than anticipated. Nights of tossing and turning in the early summer heat forced Kayla to consider maybe moving in with her mother wasn't one of her brightest ideas. Rozelle didn't have air-conditioning, and the Bay Area was experiencing a heatwave. In addition to the temperature, the mattress was too firm for her back. As hard as she tried, sound sleep eluded her half the night. She catnapped in her office for a few hours in the mornings, finding her office chair more comfortable than the bed. Plus, the store had air-conditioning.

The stress from having to hear her husband's voice on a daily basis contributed to her mental anguish. Sam insisted on calling her instead of sending a text to check up on her and the baby. The spontaneous pop-ups at the store were getting old too. Sometimes he'd bring flowers, other times, her favorite food. In Ashley's presence, she indulged him, but when he'd update her on the house renovations, she offered no input. She also played phone dodgeball with Pastor Simmons and church members who called to offer assistance with the dislocation. Dodging her mother-in-law's calls was impossible, because Mama Stella would call Rozelle's landline. According to Sam, he and Danté received home-cooked meals and offers to help replace anything that was lost in the fire. Kayla didn't like that some of the offers came from single women who were attracted to Sam, but concealed her thoughts, not wanting to give Sam hope. He was already exercising faith by declaring his love for her every single day.

The one thing Kayla did enjoy was spending time with Danté. Every evening, Sam brought him over and the two hung out like old times. She relished Danté's hugs and listening to him read to the baby. Before leaving, he always told her he loved her and asked when she was moving back with them. Her static answer was, "We'll talk about that later."

"Want me to pick you up something while I'm out? Or, is your fine husband bringing lunch today?"

Ashley's question caught her off guard. "Huh?"

"You're standing there rubbing your stomach and licking your lips, like you're hungry. I can't tell if the hunger is for food or Sam," Ashley teased.

"Girl, stop. You know it's lunch time." Kayla waved off the jesting. Ashley didn't know about the separation.

"I know, and I'm starved. I skipped dinner last night. Praise Dance rehearsal ran over."

Kayla laughed, leaning against the customer service counter. "I don't know if I'll ever get used to this church girl version."

Ashley joined with her laughter. "My mama is so happy, she cries every time she sees me."

"That's odd, because your presence brings me extreme joy."

Both Kayla and Ashley's head snapped in the direction of the baritone voice belonging to the man carrying red roses, dressed in a casual blazer and slacks.

"Hi, Bobby." Kayla nudged Ashley, whose mouth hung. "I think he's talking to you."

"You have me mixed up with someone else. My name is Leroy Jackson from North Carolina. I'm a Christian and I've been watching you, and you're someone I'd like to get to know." He extended the flowers. "Please accept these as a small token of my adoration, and allow me to escort you to lunch and I'll tell you all about me. Then if you have room in your heart to love me, we can get married, make some babies and grow old together."

Ashley and Kayla simultaneously gasped.

"Are you serious? I mean about being saved," Ashley stammered.

Kayla stepped backward as Leroy moved closer to Ashley.

Leroy stroked Ashley's cheek with his free hand. "Yes, I am. I'm in love with Jesus and I'm in love with you."

"Oh my God," Kayla mouthed.

"Hallelujah! I am so glad I was here to witness this," Sam shouted, from behind Kayla. She was so engrossed in the scene rolling before her, she didn't notice him in the store. For a brief moment they locked eyes and shared a smile.

Ashley then received the roses with tears streaming down her cheeks.

"Well, Lady Ashley, do you think I'm someone you'd like to get to know?" Leroy pressed.

"Yes." Ashley blushed.

"You only have an hour for lunch, so you better talk fast," Kayla teased. "Now get out of here and be happy," she added, almost as an afterthought.

Sam and Leroy shared a congratulatory embrace, with Sam shouting, "Thank you, Jesus!"

"I am so happy for them," Sam exclaimed, as they exited the store holding hands.

"Yeah, me too," Kayla replied, while looking for an escape. "I have customers to help. You can leave that on my desk," she said, in reference to the food container Sam was carrying, then left him standing there.

∞

"Baby, can I ask you a question?" Rozelle stood in the doorway of the spare room.

"Sure, what's up?"

"What are you doing?"

Kayla glanced up from the screen. "Right now, I'm surfing the Internet to get an idea of the current rental market."

Rozelle stepped completely in the room. "What I mean is, why are you here? I don't mind having you here, but don't you think it's time for you to join your husband and son?"

Kayla sighed and set the computer on the nightstand. "Ma, nothing has changed between Sam and I."

"And things won't change as long as you're here."

"Exactly." Kayla adjusted the back pillow. "Sam and I are through."

Rozelle broke the intense stare that followed, then sat down on the bed. "Remove the mistake both of you made with Danté and tell me exactly what unforgiveable sin did Sam commit?"

This was one conversation Kayla didn't want to have, but by her living under her mother's roof, she didn't have a choice.

"Ma, we've grown so far apart, I don't know him anymore. When Danté came he stopped being there for me. I'm not important to him anymore. We don't have anything in common anymore. The only time we're not fighting is when we're not speaking. He said some mean things to me, I'm sure he doesn't love me anymore." She exaggerated a little, but she wanted Rozelle to drop the subject. "And he told me if I'm unhappy to leave, so I did."

Rozelle's head shook with that stern reprimand look Kayla remembered from childhood. "Really? Well, at least Sam has the courage to admit his shortcomings."

Kayla wasn't expecting that. "What did he tell you?"

"Probably the same words he told you. The only difference is, he's not a spoiled brat that has to have his way."

Kayla really wasn't expecting that shot. "What does that have to do with anything?"

Rozelle patted Kayla's leg. "Sweetheart, I need you to forgive me. You're my only daughter. I love you, but I reared you to be a spoiled adult who can't handle not being the center of attention." She ignored Kayla's gasped and continued. "After your father died, Carlos grew up fast and made it his mission to protect his baby sister and spoiled you even more. We gave you everything you wanted, and because of that, you equate love with being the center of attention and getting your way."

Kayla stopped just short of smacking her lips. "That is so not true."

"Yes, it is," Rozelle insisted. "I saw it years ago with Candace but assumed you would grow out of it."

"Candace?" Kayla whispered her childhood friend's name. Her heart still ached for the lost.

"You and Candace bragged about someday becoming Olympic figure-skating gold medalists. Remember?"

Kayla nodded.

"Think back. In the beginning Candace liked dancing more than skating and wanted to try ballet. When she told you that, you stopped talking to her after you informed her being best friends meant doing what made you happy. You didn't speak to her until she agreed to sign up for ice skating."

Kayla had forgotten all about that bump in their friendship. "That was a long time ago, and I was a kid."

"True. So, what's your excuse now?"

Kayla wanted so much to roll her eyes, but couldn't with her mother staring her down.

"You did the same thing to Sam when he refused to date you in your boycott Jesus days. It wasn't until you had a real experience with the Lord before you acknowledged he was right." Rozelle took a deep breath. "Sweetheart, you can't continue to cut people off because they don't do what you want, or act the way you think they should. Your way is not always best, and everyone is entitled to make a mistake. Being reared by a single mother didn't provide you with an example of a healthy marital relationship. You were too young when your father died to remember the many arguments we had about his drinking. You don't know how I covered his weaknesses, and at the same time honored him as the head of our home. I'd be hurt and angry, but I always forgave him because I knew his heart was right and he loved me. He didn't fully know how to be a good husband and bear the pain of his upbringing, but he tried." She paused, as if allowing the words to sink in. "Sam is not the perfect husband. You're not the perfect wife. Both of you are feeling your way through and learning each other in addition to parenting an adolescent, while expecting a child. That's a lot for anyone. To make matters worse, you and Sam considered yourselves know-it-alls and refused help from those who love you with experience. Both of you share equal responsibility for the state of your marriage."

This time Kayla did roll her eyes and look away.

"Roll your eyes all you want, it's the truth. You left your husband because he didn't do things the way you thought he should. You didn't allow him to make mistakes and grow. Instead of supporting him and trying to understand, you checked out. You left the home where your name is on the deed. For the life of me, I can't understand that one. Sam made some poor decisions and said some things he shouldn't have, but so did you. Once Pastor Simmons pointed out his shortcomings, Sam humbled himself and admitted his faults and has done nothing but beg for your forgiveness. He's in counseling while you're still whining about sharing him with Danté. I have a newsflash for you: You married a future pastor. You and the kids will always be his first priority, but you will share him."

Her jaw fell. Kayla hadn't considered that. She also didn't know Pastor Simmons was involved.

"It's time for you to grow up," Rozelle said, standing to her feet. "Sam loves you; give him grace to grow and learn to love you in the way you can receive. Offer him the same grace he's giving you by learning to support him in a way that builds him up. Besides, there is no way on Earth you will ever let Sam live happily ever after with another woman in your house."

Her chest heaved and her eyes burned, but Kayla didn't offer a rebuttal as her mother left the room.

Chapter 31

Sam groggily patted around the bed in search of his ringing cell phone. Once he got his bearings, he remembered he'd left it charging on the dresser drawer. By the time he sat up, the personalized ringtone had stopped, only to start again. He wasn't dreaming. He jumped to his feet, grabbed his phone and panicked.

"Kayla, is it time?" he yelled into the phone. "Are you in labor?"

"No, I," she panted.

He cut her off. "I'm on my way, just as soon as I wake up Danté." He circled the room in search of his pants, while calling for Danté to wake up. "Are you on the way to the hospital or still at Mom's."

"I'm at the front door." Her heavy breathing came across staticky.

Sam stopped short of inserting his leg into the pants. Maybe he was dreaming. "You're where?"

"I'm at the front door." More panting. "Hurry up and open the door."

With the pants in hand, Sam sprinted to the front door and swung it open. He wasn't dreaming, Kayla was there dancing on the porch.

She brushed past him inside. "I gotta pee, where's the bathroom?"

Bewildered, Sam pointed toward the hallway. "First door on the right." In her haste, she nearly knocked Danté down as he came down the same hallway.

"What's going on?" Danté asked, still in pajamas, rubbing his eyes.

"I have no idea," Sam answered truthfully. There had to be a logical reason why Kayla chose to drive across town after 2:00 a.m. to use the bathroom. He just didn't know what it was. He used the arm of the couch for support, trying to wake up and figure it out. By the time his heart rate slowed to normal and he attempted again to step into his pants, she returned.

She breathed relief. "Woo, that feels so much better. Sometimes it feels like this girl is sitting right on my bladder." She smiled.

Sam didn't understand, she stood there rubbing her stomach and checking out the room layout like her actions were totally normal. When she went on a self-guided tour of the apartment, he looked over at Danté, who was now standing beside him, and they both shrugged their shoulders.

"This place is more spacious than I thought," she announced, back in the living room. "The bathroom is a little small, but the bedrooms are big." Her face twisted as she retraced her steps down the hallway and back again. "Where's the PlayStation?"

Sam smirked. "You're kidding, right? After the stunts he pulled, this boy may not play video games until he's thirty."

Danté sighed and plopped down on the couch.

A nervous giggle escaped her lips and Sam's heart lurched inside his chest, but he remained still, studying her. She was so beautiful with her curly ponytail and rubbing the mound that housed their child. It seemed like an eternity since he'd heard her laugh.

"When I heard your voice on the phone, I thought you were in early labor." He hoped the statement would lead her into voicing the thoughts enclosed in her pretty little head.

She waved off his concern. "I'm only thirty-two weeks. Unless she decides to come early, we have at least eight weeks to go. Hopefully, by that time we'll be back in our home. Oh, before I forget, I saw the new cabinets I want on HGTV."

We? Our? Sam swallowed hard, in an effort to remain calm. What was his drama queen saying?

Danté stood and yawned. "I'm going back to bed. Goodnight, little brother," he added, patting Kayla's stomach as he passed by. "I'll see you in the morning."

Sam remained fixated on her as the nervous giggles returned, accompanied by pacing. "I'm glad to see you, but this two a.m. wake-up call is throwing me off. What's on your mind? It must be important because this is the most you've said to me since," he paused and looked down, "since the night you left."

She ceased pacing, and threw her hands up facing him. "Look, you knew I was a drama queen when you married me, so work with me here. I'll work on that later, one thing at a time. Right now, I need to tell you something. I won't be able to sleep until I do."

"I'm listening."

She positioned herself in front of him, as close as her stomach would allow, then took several deep breaths. "Sam, husband, I forgive you. I heard you in the car, and I forgive you. I know it was never your intention to hurt me. I shouldn't have left. In my anger, I said some mean things to you that I didn't mean and then I left. That was wrong."

Sam felt his lips part, but he knew better than to interrupt now. There was more to come.

She stepped back, wringing her hands. "I haven't always supported you with the right motives. To be honest, the majority of the time my support was given as a means to get my way, not out of love. Husband, please forgive me." Her lips trembled. "I am a spoiled brat, but I am no longer a child. I'm a grown woman, a wife and mother. It's time for me to grow up and accept the world doesn't revolve around me and my desires. Wait! Let me finish," she interjected when he stood up. "I need to say this. I have been so miserable since I left, and not just because of the heat. In my stubbornness, I've been trying to convince myself that I don't need you, but that's a lie. Just like you want to learn how to be the husband I need, I want to be the wife you need. I'm sure it will take a whole lot of counseling for me to learn how to control my tongue, but I'm willing to put in the work for us. I miss how close we used to be. No matter what I said in the past, you are the best the part of my life. That's the real reason I want to have a baby; to have part of you forever. I love you."

Her visibly trembling body conveyed how much the vulnerability cost her. Kayla coming to him on her own terms in the wee hours of the morning was worth the hours spent in prayer and counseling. He went to reach for her, but realized he was still holding his pants. He wrapped his arms around her waist after tossing his pants on the couch. "Come here." He needed to hold her close, but her protruding abdomen prevented him. Refusing to be denied, he interlocked their fingers and after sitting back down, settled her on his lap, cuddling with her head resting against his chest. "I beg to differ, you're the best part of me. You can get angry and yell, curse me out, or even hit me. Whatever you have to do, just don't ever leave again. My heart can't handle that."

After raising her head and making eye contact, she whispered, "I won't."

He leaned down and hoped his trembling kiss would convey the depths of his love for her. At her soft moan, he deepened the kiss, all the while inwardly thanking God for restoring his marriage. He held her until the warmth from her body reminded him, he wasn't dressed. He ended the dance with her lips and kissed her forehead.

"Are you hungry? Give me a minute; I can heat up some leftovers." He reached for his pants.

She grabbed his hand and licked her lower lip before answering. "I'm famished. Why get dressed? You look good in boxers and even better without them."

For a moment, Sam stared at her, amazed, before laughter poured from him. After maneuvering to his feet with Kayla in his arms, he started toward the hallway.

"Wait, where are you going and what are you going to do?"

Her innocent seduction tactic was too cute and never got old. "I'm going to do what I enjoy most, take you to bed and spoil you rotten."

∞

Ten weeks later

Kayla ignored the noise and cuddled closer to Sam, determined to sleep in at least once this month. Her plan failed when Sam turned onto his side and began shaking her.

"Babe, it's time to wake up."

"No," she whined. "It's your turn."

"No, I got up last time."

The noise intensified.

"That's okay, I'll get the baby," Danté announced.

Kayla opened her eyes and tilted her head up. She hadn't heard Danté enter their room, but there he was standing over the basinet. He was the perfect big brother, always offering to help.

After an exasperated breath, Kayla conceded her quest for sleep and sat completely up. "It's close to feeding time, I'd better get up." She nudged Sam. "Come on, partner. If I have to get up, then so do you. I need a diaper."

Sam grunted and turned over, but instead of sitting up, rested on his elbow.

"Here it is. The wipes too and the white creamy stuff." Danté thrust them in her face. "Can I pick out the outfit today?"

The expectant eyes and grin nearly bought her to tears. She'd never seen Danté this happy, not even before Sherri passed away. Counseling and Pastor Simmons' strong hand was teaching them how to love as a family unit without being motivated by past hurts. Each member was secure in their role. Sam and Kayla were also learning how to ask for and accept help from their extended family.

"Sure." She narrowed her eyes at Sam. "You're more of a help than your father is this morning."

"And I'm perfectly okay with that," Sam admitted. A strong nudge later he sat completely up and stole a kiss before Danté placed the baby in Kayla's arms. "Too bad you didn't get what you wanted this time."

Kayla smiled at the men in her life and then down at the bundle in her arms. "No, God didn't give me what I wanted, but He definitely gave me what I needed." With total contentment she kissed her baby boy's forehead. The growing pains of the past year were more than worth it.

Discussion Questions

1. Sam and Kayla were married two years and trying to conceive. How long should married couples wait before having children?
2. Sam and Kayla were both reared by single mothers. How do you think this factored into how they viewed marital relationships?
3. Kayla was spoiled and use to having things her way. Do you think parents should spoil their children? In which circumstances should parents say no?
4. Sam and Kayla depended on books to learn about child-rearing. Do you think this was a wise decision? What role, if any, should books play in child-rearing?
5. Should couples discuss child-rearing philosophies before marriage?
6. What role, if any, should therapists play in helping children deal with the loss of a parent?
7. Did Sam's jealousy of Pastor Simmons' role in Kayla's life surprise you?
8. How can young couples, especially those in the ministry, balance marriage and parenting?

More titles by Wanda B. Campbell:

First Sunday in October – Simone Family Series Book 1
Games - Simone Family Series Book 2
Liberation - Simone Family Series Book 3
Unresolved Issues - Simone Family Series Book 4
Illusions
Right Package, Wrong Baggage
Silver Lining
Doin' Me
Back to Me
Under the Influence
Kayla's Redemption – Journey Series Book 1